Autumn's Attack

By C. M. Stolworthy

Autumn's Attack

Book 2 of the
Seasons Series

C.M. Stolworthy

This edition published in 2023
by Maida Vale Publishing,
An imprint of The Black Spring Press Group,
London, United Kingdom

Typeset by Subash Raghu
Graphic design by @padrondesign

ISBN 978-1-915406-21-7
www.blackspringpressgroup.com

CHAPTER ONE

Laran looked up from his maps as Lord Aristata sauntered in. His posture relaxed as he avoided eye contact with Laran, making Laran laugh.

'Stop laughing and get that mind out of the gutter,' Aristata grumbled as he walked gracefully over to the table where the plans for the latest campaign were spread. Leaning his six-foot-four frame over the study, his dark eyes scrunched at the corners in concentration as he determinedly ignored Laran.

'Okay. Spit it out,' James droned, glancing at his friend and superior, as he ran his hand through his short, cropped auburn hair.

'Why so defensive, James?' Laran chuckled, enjoying teasing his friend.

'What do you mean, why? You've been ribbing me about this girl ever since I met her at that damn party *you* forced me to attend.'

'Forced is strong,' Laran complained teasingly.

'Okay, she finally agreed to a second date, and it went well,' Aristata bent down to study a map of the stronghold, holding his breath while he waited for Laran to join the dots.

'Finally got past first base then?' Laran nudged his friend's shoulder playfully.

'Oh, um, yeah,' James replied. A small smile flashed across his features as he feigned interest in the battle plans spread across the table.

'Does that mean I'm finally going to get to meet her, then?' Laran asked.

'Maybe one day,' James answered, his expression sheepish.

'Why all the secrecy? We're friends, aren't we? You're being so cloak and dagger about this mystery lady of yours. I'm thinking you're making her up.'

Lord Aristata was serene. 'You'll get to meet her... Eventually. It's just that... you know you're a big scary fella. The last thing I need is you scaring her off. Besides, remember that little blonde I introduced to you? One look at you and I didn't even register,' James huffed, crossing his arms over his chest.

'What's that supposed to mean? I'll have you know I can be the perfect gentleman... When

I want to be.' Laran shrugged with a look of mock hurt.

'Hmm... A likely story, anyway look sharp the boss is coming,' Lord Aristata said as Mother Nature entered the command tent.

'What are you two slackers chuckling about?' Holly asked as she walked over to Laran and put her arm around his waist, kissing him on the cheek as she did so.

'Jimmy here is about to reveal the identity of his mystery girlfriend.' Laran announced with a cheeky grin. 'You know full well who she is,' James laughed as Laran kissed Holly back.

'Oh, get a room you two!' said Ash as he walked into the tent. Laran grinned at him. He looked tired, with slight bags under his eyes and not his usual cocky self.

'That baby keeping you up then, Ash?' Laran enquired, watching a huge smile spread across Ash's face.

'Sure is, the little rascal, and I get massive brownie points if I get him down at night,' he winked at the others, making them chuckle. 'Heard you met Jasmine's family. How did that go?'

'Oh, you know awkward as you would expect, I am not quite what her father had in mind for a son-in-law. Who told you?' James chuckled as a blush crept up his neck.

'Oh, erm Lord Alloces, the girls are friends… You know what it's like. What with the babies and stuff,' he shrugged.

'Of course, shame. The rest of us aren't as united as you Spring Elves. Then maybe we wouldn't be doing this again,' James mused as Holly gave him a sympathetic smile.

'How's Ana?' Holly asked, brightly changing the subject. She liked the Springs and felt Lord Aristata needed a diversion.

'Still messing with that rock star?'

'Yeah, cocky bastard, hoping she takes him down a peg or two.' Ash chuckled. 'Bought her a château last month, been holed up there ever since.'

'Right then! Are we doing this?' James enquired, still grinning. 'I for one am certain that Lord Eriator is in there and once we've got him, we can nip this minor rebellion in the bud.'

'Alright ladies, enough socialising. We have a job to do. I've just spoken to Alectrona and her man on the inside has assured her that the Dark Elf Emperor is definitely in the castle,' Holly said, her expression serious.

'How certain is Alectrona that her man is trustworthy? It wouldn't be the first false lead we've had recently,' Ash asked.

'She's positive. Apparently her spy is high up in the Dark Elf pecking order and is possibly even a lord,' Holly reassured him.

Ash studied the map. 'Exactly how certain are you? It's going to be very costly capturing this place. I'm not sure we can afford it if it turns out to be an expensive ruse.'

'Yes, I'm sure, Alectrona's man on the inside assured her he is definitely there,' Aristata replied.

'Yes, well, I'm not too thrilled to be trusting Alectrona on this one. After all, she won't even tell us who this Dark Elf spy of hers is,' Ash replied.

'Alectrona assured me her man was well placed.'

'He must be. From what I've heard, things are falling apart in the Dark Elf camp. The Emperor's generals have realised that the end is near. Apparently, there have been two attempts on the Emperor's life this year alone. He's had to move around a lot to stay ahead of the dissidents, let alone us,' James Aristata said.

'I'm certain this is the one. The moment news got out that we had the castle surrounded, a large Dark Elf force rushed up to aid them. Anahuit intercepted them and is currently engaging them around a small town twenty miles south of here. Even if the Emperor isn't inside, this place must be important for them to respond like that,' Holly replied.

'Well, alright then, how do we get in to find out for certain?' Ash asked with anticipation.

'That's where I come in,' Laran said as he leaned over a large map of the Dark Elf stronghold on the table.

'The Emperor had holed up in a classic medieval castle town. Because of the strong possibility that there are plenty of civilians inside, we will not be using artillery to crack the nut I'm afraid. I've brought up a force of trolls to break through the castle front gates into the city. Lord Aristata and I will lead the vanguard with them. We'll fight our way through the city to the main fortress complex.' Laran studied the faces before him.

'Seems like the best plan. FERA wants him alive if that is possible,' Holly smirked as Laran rolled his eyes.

'That settles it then,' Laran declared with a grin, 'I will lead my men over the walls with the grappling hooks and capture the gate house. Once it's open, you will bring your men up to assist me, Aristata, and help me secure the courtyard. Assuming we still have a fighting force after that, Ash's troops will link up with us and we'll storm the keep. Agreed?'

'Agreed.' Ash, Aristata and Holly said together before streaming out of the tent to make the final preparations.

The castle was heavily defended, and the fighting was fierce. Laran took the first wave of troops and, using grappling hooks, they scaled the walls before securing the gate from the other side without too much trouble. Right on cue, Aristata led his men rushing through the narrow entryway to join him. 'Are you secure here?' he panted, getting his breath back.

'Yeah, just about,' Laran managed. He could feel pain.

'You're bleeding Laran! Where are you hurt?' Aristata scanned his body, concerned he could see a lot of blood.

'It's fine, just a scratch. It looks worse than it is.'

'Okay if you're sure,' Aristata said, still concerned about his state, 'Ash and Holly are in already. They found a poster gate and blasted their way through.'

Laran looked up with alarm. That wasn't the plan, damn that woman. He took a deep breath and blocked out the pain.

'Better get in there then,' Laran managed heading toward the entrance, six of his best warriors flanking him.

What met him inside was shocking. The castle was littered with bodies of fallen combatants and the corridors were thick with smoke.

'Ah! King Autumn,' echoed a calm and sinister voice through the halls, '...At last. So good of you to join us,' a tall, Dark Elf smiled evilly at him. He nodded his head slightly and another group of Dark Elves moved forward, neutralising Laran's guard and taking hold of Aristata, dragging him forward and forcing him to kneel.

'What do you want?' Laran snarled, realising too late.

He had led his men into a trap.

The Dark Elves had been warned.

He had been betrayed.

The Dark Elf circled Laran with his hands clasped behind his back, studying his enemy as he struggled to get free. 'Getting right to the point, are we, Laran?' he retorted, satisfied with the success of his plan as he crouched down in front of him. Icy fingers clasped Laran's cheeks and jerked his head up. The Elf reeked of death, and his crimson eyes invaded Laran's soul. '*I want* the elder council crushed and *I WANT* this planet back!' he listed. He was calm and deadly. '...And without you I can remove the Human vermin once and for all,' he answered, all the while smiling. Two of the Elves yanked up King Spring's body and dragged it forward, dumping it on the ground in front of Laran.

'Your brother,' the Elf smiled coldly as he nodded his head. They dragged Holly forward. She was barely conscious. Laran's eyes opened wide with shock as the elf calmly stabbed her through the heart, dropping her next to Ash.

'Oh, dear. Did I just kill Mother Nature?' He stared at Laran coldly, smirking as he slowly walked towards him.

'I can't kill you, but I can make this hurt, make you scream for death, just like you did to my family. Do you remember them? No, didn't think so.' He casually dragged the blade of his sword down Laran's body before stabbing him in the thigh, dropping him to the ground. Taking a handful of Laran's hair, he pulled his head up, forcing Laran to look him in the eye.

'Your disgusting Elves attack my home on the pretence of looking for weapons,' he spat every word with pain and hatred. 'We had no weapons. We were a peaceful farming community. Once you had slaughtered all the old men, as that was who was defending the village, you went for women and children.'

'Your men rounded up the women. They took my wife and forced my young son to watch. *Watch...* as his mother begged for mercy. And do you know? When they finished they turned on my innocent child. Then they torched the village so I could find no evidence. They were sloppy, your men, and there were survivors to speak of such barbarism.' Smiling, he ran Laran through, enjoying the pain on his face. 'If one day you have a son,' he snarled, 'I will hunt him down and I will make you suffer like I did, you will know how it feels to know you failed and that you couldn't save them.' Rising to his feet he casually turned and walked away from the carnage that now littered the floor.

'Goodbye King Autumn. Might see you around,' he laughed as he stepped over Laran's body, viciously clubbing Aristata on his way out, knocking him to the floor, unconscious.

CHAPTER TWO

PRESENT DAY

Willow and Jacen wandered down to the river to see if the Water Sprite had appeared again. They sat on the riverbank, took off their socks and shoes, and dipped their feet into the stream.

'I love it down here,' Willow murmured. 'It's so peaceful – and William isn't here moaning every five seconds.' Willow grinned and tentatively rested her hand on Jacen's.

'No twins either.' Jacen laid back and closed his eyes, making sure not to move his hand. 'I love him to bits but,' Willow paused to find the right words, 'he can be so whiny sometimes.'

Willow lay back, now touching his arm with hers. 'This is the first time I've been allowed out since the kidnapping. I've missed you.' Willow took a deep, cleansing breath, letting the fresh air fill her lungs.

'Yeah. Mum kept me in for two whole days and when she let me out, I had to stay on the farm. I thought I was going to go mad,' Jacen replied as he chewed a piece of grass.

'Sorry about that. Our mums seem to have entered some sort of alliance against us.'

Heli skipped merrily down towards the edge of the stream. Sheila, the Sprite, waited for her, camouflaged amongst the tangled knots of plant life that clogged the riverbanks each summer.

'Hi!' Sheila greeted.

'Hello… erm…' Heli struggled.

'Sheila.'

'Oh, Sheila's a lovely name!' Heli beamed.

'I heard all about your escapades at the castle last week,' Sheila said.

'Oh, really? How?' Heli asked.

'The tree Sprites that rescued you – well, they are quite famous in Scotland now because of it!'

Jacen sat up and wiped the sweat off his forehead, pushing his hair out of his face. 'I'm far too hot sitting here. I think I might paddle in the stream and talk to Sheila for a bit.'

'Oh, okay,' Willow released his hand and watched Jacen wade across the stream to the Sprite.

Occasionally, the Sprite would ask Jacen a question and she would often giggle at his replies, doing tricks like jumping into the air and flipping like a dolphin. After a while, Heli walked over and flopped down next to Willow, leaving Jacen with Sheila.

'Were you and Jacen holding hands just now?' Heli asked, trying not to smile.

'No, not really. Well, sort of,' Willow answered. Heli sat up.

'What do you mean, sort of?' Heli paused and glanced at Willow, noticing she seemed subdued.

'What's up?' Heli smiled, and her eyes twinkled. 'You're jealous!' she declared with confidence.

'What! Jealous of whom?' Willow frowned. 'Sheila?'

'You're jealous of Sheila for talking to Jacen.' Heli's smile spread across her face and her eyes lit up with triumph as she crossed her arms over her chest. Willow's eyes filled with tears as she looked away, trying not to cry.

'Oh, Willow! I'm sorry. I didn't mean to tease you! Tell me what's wrong!'

'Oh Heli, it's not just Sheila — it's everything. Even at school, Jacen's popular with the girls and he just doesn't see me. I know we're always together, but it's like he doesn't see me as anything other than me. But when I look at him…' Willow turned away and fiddled with a piece of grass.

'I see your problem now,' Heli said.

'You do?'

'Yeah,' Heli said. 'You guys are friends, but if you tell him you like him, he might freak out and stop hanging out with you.'

'So, what do I do?'

'I have absolutely no idea,' Heli said.

'Thank you, Heli, for yet another pearl of your infinite wisdom!'

'You're welcome,' Heli retorted.

'Anyway, how's Guardian Elf School going?' Willow asked, changing the subject. She sat crossed legged, getting more comfortable.

'Oh, it's cool — I'm getting quite good at close quarters combat. The other day I almost broke a Winter Elf's arm!' Heli replied, her face lighting up with glee. 'Those Winter Elves are so up themselves.'

'Heli, I'm not sure you're supposed to be this happy at the thought of causing someone serious physical harm,' Willow replied.

'Huh. Maybe not, but oh well!' Heli grinned cheekily before getting up to talk to Sheila again. For a moment, Willow was alone with her thoughts until Jacen came over and sat down next to her.

'So... How was that shopping trip the other day?' Willow asked, trying to sound casual.

'Awful! It took ages thanks to the twins and once they'd finally decided on a pair of shoes they liked, they wanted to go clothes shopping. It was torture! I'd rather bite off my arm than do it again. How was your day with William? Was he still grumpy?' Jacen asked with a grin.

'Oh! Yeah, he was fine in the morning and Mum stayed home from work. I think she felt guilty about the whole thing. We did some online shopping because she feels underdressed at work and apparently everyone else is always dressed so smart. I think she should spend less time around the Elves. It's not natural that they're so good looking! William played on his games console with Heli. She's getting great at it, which is annoying William a lot…'

'Hey Jacen, do you want to help me catch crayfish?' Sheila's voice suddenly interrupted their conversation as she shouted at them from across the stream.

'Sure,' he replied, before getting up and running back down to the water's edge.

'You know the American ones are the best. I don't feel as guilty about eating them because they were an introduced species,' Sheila informed him.

Jacen listened and nodded in agreement.

'They were encroaching on the habitat of the native ones, which are smaller and more polite in my experience,' Sheila added.

'Interesting,' Jacen muttered. 'I wouldn't know.'

Sheila caught one and held it up to show Jacen. 'The American ones are aggressive as well and really should be removed from the stream when found,' Sheila advised proudly and dropped a crayfish into her mouth, crunching on it loudly. Jacen's faced paled, and he looked to Willow like he might be sick. Willow laughed from the bank, clutching her aching stomach as her eyes started watering.

'Oh, my!' Sheila said, turning to Willow. 'Are you melting or leaking?' Sheila stared at Willow as Jacen burst out laughing.

'No, no, I'm fine really,' Willow managed, wiping the tears off her face. 'It's getting late, we should probably go,' she announced as she climbed to her feet.

'Oh, alright,' said the Sprite.

'Bye Sheila, it was nice seeing you again,' said Jacen with a wave.

'It was nice seeing you!' she shouted before diving under the eddying surface of the water. With a kick of her tail, she shot off upstream.

Jacen casually took Willow's hand as they walked away from the riverbank after Heli.

'The twins have been learning sign language.'

'Really, why?' asked Heli.

'I don't know, but they've been discussing William a lot lately.'

'I bet they're gonna wind him right up!' Willow chuckled with glee.

'Did you just do an evil chuckle?' Jacen laughed.

'Maybe,' Willow replied, her voice high-pitched and sheepish.

'What are you doing tomorrow?' asked Jacen.

'I think we're going to Gran's tomorrow,' Willow said as they stopped by the garden gate.

'Okay, how about a bike ride this weekend?'

'Yeah, alright – Mum might have got over her 'stay near the house' rule by then,' replied Willow. She was about to open the gate when Jacen said her name.

Willow turned around. 'What Jace –?'

He leaned forward and kissed her gently. He pulled away and smiled, blushing slightly. Willow took his hand and smiled back.

★★★

'But I don't want to go!' William signed furiously at David, as Willow entered the kitchen for breakfast. 'You can't make me! That's not fair!' William complained, sitting on a chair, and crossing his arms impetuously.

'Come on, William. Be reasonable. You know you can't stay here on your own – not after Sunday's incident. I'm sorry, but I must go to work, and Mum's already gone – so you have to go to Gran's,' David reasoned.

Willow sat down next to William to eat her cereal. She found the heated, but silent argument amusing. 'What's wrong with Gran's house?' she asked through a mouthful of cereal.

'She has no television. That's what's wrong!' William signed. 'So, I can't play on my game console, and I'm not allowed out.'

'You are allowed out. I just said you couldn't go into town with Tom, that's all,' David sighed as William ignored him.

'What, may I ask, are we going to do all flipping week?' William pouted. 'It's bad enough that I've been a prisoner in my own home because Mum thinks I'm bloody 'delicate'. I even had to put up with those twins yesterday because they all came over for tea. One of them tried to kiss me! Got me cornered so I couldn't even run away! I don't even know which one it was!'

Willow and Heli turned away so he couldn't see them giggle.

'William, for goodness' sake, you're not supposed to run away. You're supposed to enjoy the attention of two pretty girls,' David laughed as William glared at him.

'Well, I'm sure Gran has organised something for us to do anyway,' Willow said, trying to hide her smile. William turned his glare towards her.

'Oh great! I can't wait!' said William, his voice dripping with sarcasm.

'Anyway. Hurry up, Willow! You have one hour to get ready and then I'm driving both of you over there,' David said as he left for the study.

'This is entirely your fault,' William signed at Willow.

'Whatever, William,' she scoffed. 'I don't know why you're making such a fuss. I should have left you at that castle,' Willow said through Heli. She couldn't be bothered to sign. 'I'm going to get dressed.' Willow stood up, put her cereal bowl in the sink, and stomped back upstairs.

The drive to Gran's was a silent affair. William sat on his hands, refusing to look at anyone, and David focused on the road. They were all rather relieved when they turned into the drive.

★★★

Althea paced around the office she shared with Lilly. Occasionally, she glanced out the large window, concentrating on the dilemma they had found themselves in. However, Lilly simply stared at the wall; the window was too much of a distraction. She twiddled the memory stick with her fingers, trying to decide what exactly to do next.

'I don't know what to do, Althea,' Lilly said telepathically. Althea hopped onto the desk and took a handful of paper clips, carefully building a tower out of them.

'Oh! I just remembered,' Althea said, her eyes widening as a smile crept across her face. 'You know that cute young man we saw with King Autumn the other day?' Althea asked.

'Yes… What about him?' Lilly replied without talking.

'He is an Elf,' Althea said as she tidied the paper clips around her tower. 'I meant to tell you sooner, but it slipped my mind.'

'Really? Are you sure?' Lilly asked, arching a brow in surprise. 'He looked pretty human to me.'

'I'm pretty sure – although I haven't seen one like him in a long time. He looked like an Autumn Elf, which was probably why you didn't recognise him.' Althea stood back, admiring her tower.

'That's interesting. I don't think I've ever met an Autumn Elf before.'

'There aren't many left. They fought for Laran in the last Dark Elf uprising and sadly, most of them got killed,' Althea said, the corners of her mouth drooping and her eyes misting up.

'That really was awful,' Lilly replied as a moment of silence stretched between them. 'I wonder if he's here now.' Lilly pushed herself out of her chair and hurried to the door. Althea followed her, her paperclip tower collapsing behind her.

Lilly walked down the fluorescent lit corridor, past the water cooler and the plant collection that was tastefully arranged in an alcove, and past all the offices with their glass doors. She looked into every office she passed, until she found Gail in the last office at the end of the corridor, sitting at his desk and sipping coffee while reading something on his computer screen. His suit jacket hung on the back of his chair.

'Knock! Knock!' Lilly smiled from the door.

'Oh! Hello, Mother Nature – come in,' he smiled. Lilly entered and sat down.

'He's well informed,' Althea commented telepathically as she sat on the chair next to Lilly.

'So he is,' Lilly replied telepathically while still smiling at Gail.

'I'm Gail,' he said. 'I don't think we've ever properly met, and I've never met your Guardian Elf.'

'I'm Althea.'

'How may I help you?'

'I'm sorry, you seem to know who I am – but I have no idea who you are – and I know all my staff. Who hired you?' Lilly asked in a polite but professional manner.

'Erm, okay,' he said, feeling flustered by her stern attitude. 'Well, my full name is Gaillardia Autumn, but most people call me Gail. I'm here to help King Autumn with general admin. He hired me a month ago, just for the summer. That's pretty much all there is to tell.'

'Wow!' Althea squeaked from her chair. 'You *are* an Autumn Elf!'

Gail nodded, a slight smile tugging at the corners of his mouth, before returning his attention to Lilly.

'Hang on,' Althea asked. 'Did you say your last name was Autumn?'

'I did.'

'Hmm Gaillardia Autumn… I knew a Gaillardia once. He was the son of Lord James Aristata of the Autumn Council.' Althea narrowed her eyes.

'I think I should go get my dad. I mean King Autumn,' Gail stuttered, blushing.

'Althea,' Lilly said. 'What are you talking about?'

'You are Lord Aristata! Wow, I never thought that rumour was true,' Althea started scrutinising Gail's face, making him blush even more.

'Althea, what are you talking about?' Lilly demanded.

'Gail's father, Lord Aristata, was one of Laran's commanders. He was a brilliant strategist,' Althea explained. 'It was a massive blow to the Autumn Elves and King Laran when the Dark Elves killed him and his family.' Althea looked at Gail. Curiosity flickered across her face. 'Except you, I suppose. Are you the only survivor? Your dad?'

'No one else survived. Only me.' Gail's voice was devoid of emotion.

'So, you are Gaillardia Aristata, aren't you? Not Autumn.'

Gail nodded. Colour filled his cheeks.

'Oh – that's interesting,' Lilly said and paused, looking at Gail and Althea, unsure how to go on.

'Have I done something wrong?' asked Gail, clearing his throat.

'No, you haven't. But you're an Elf pretending to be a Human. Why is that?' Lilly narrowed her eyes at him.

'Well, yes. I am an Elf,' he said. 'But I'm not sure where you're going with this. I'm not pretending to be anything.' Gail frowned.

'Well, most of the people working here know about Elves – and most of the Elves working here are pretty conspicuous. So why bother pretending?'

'I do like working here and the more Human I appear, the easier it is for me to be accepted and get promoted. I'm not pretending.' Gail crossed his arms defensively as he replied, 'I always look like this.'

'Possibly,' Lilly shot back, her voice cold. 'So, you say King Laran hired you? Why? He doesn't normally hire staff here. Why are you really here?'

Gail's cheeks felt hot as the implications of her words filtered through his brain. 'Are you accusing me of something?' Gail spluttered. 'If there is nothing else I can help you with, perhaps you ought to leave!'

'We'll leave when we're good and ready,' Lilly replied icily.

Gail let out a long sigh, and Lilly looked at him. She could see it rattled him. In fact, his expression reminded her of Willow and William when they had been caught doing something wrong. She exhaled heavily. *He's just a boy,* she thought.

'He is Lord Aristata of the Third House of Autumn Elves. He is not likely to be a spy,' Althea said to Lilly telepathically.

'I'll ask again – who do you work for?' Lilly asked, softening her tone.

'Okay – look!' Gail said, 'I'm not the spy you're after. Yes, I work for King Autumn, and he knows about a spy as well. He asked me to find out who it is. The people I work with don't know who my parents are, or that King Autumn is my father.'

'Is King Autumn here now?' Lilly asked.

'Yes, he's in his office,' Gail replied, his voice sullen.

'Well, now we've got to the bottom of that, I need to talk to him.'

Laran was on the phone when Lilly marched in without invitation. He held up a silencing finger as he finished his conversation. This did not improve Lilly's mood.

'Yes, I'm aware of that... No, she is here now... No, it's fine, I'll handle it,' he said curtly before placing the phone down.

'Lilly, what a pleasant surprise!' Laran said as he stood up and smiled at her politely. His office was sparsely furnished: it contained an empty desk and chair, two spare ones against the wall, and a filing cabinet which stood forlornly in a corner. On the walls hung two bland landscapes. Laran pulled out the two chairs for his guests.

'I'm not here for small talk, Laran. I have some questions regarding that Autumn Elf who's been following you around.'

'Gail? Yes, he was just on the phone with me. Apparently, you've been giving him the full third degree,' Laran joked.

'Tell me, King Autumn, Gail – is he actually Aristata's son?' Althea asked.

Laran's smile dissolved. 'Yes, he is,' he said at last.

'I heard that was the worst massacre in Elven history. It's amazing he survived at all. How many people know he exists?' Althea asked.

'Very few – and I would prefer it if it stayed that way,' Laran said. 'It was a massacre. Queen Andarta found him… She was one of the first on the scene.' Laran sat back in his chair, his voice hushed.

'Don't worry,' Althea reassured him. 'I'll make sure Gail's safe.'

Laran appraised the little Elf. 'I'm impressed,' he said. 'Very few people would recognise him or even remember his father,' Laran said.

'Yes, well, he favours his mother. He looks a lot like his grandfather,' Althea said. 'Bringing him here, though – is that safe?'

'Yes, I think so,' said Laran. 'There are very few people or Elves left that would remember or even recognise him and certainly none here – apart from Hurleston and Hàlfr – but they know, anyway. How else would we have hidden him?'

'I take it when you say hidden, you mean he was brought up as a Human in the Human world?' Althea asked.

'Yes, Annie thought he would be safer away from the Elves.'

Althea nodded in understanding. Laran relaxed and turned his attention back to Lilly, who was watching the exchange with knitted brows.

'We still haven't gotten to the bottom of why you were interrogating my boy. Are you usually so aggressive with HR?' Laran asked with a smirk.

'Laran, you should have informed me your son was working in the department,' Lilly admonished. 'We deal with a lot of sensitive information here and I'm worried we have a leak.'

'And you think it's Gail?'

'Well, I try to have at least a passing knowledge of all the staff working here. So, to see someone I didn't know wandering around was slightly disconcerting,' Lilly replied.

'Yes, I'm sorry about that. But, you see, it was all part of my plan. I've been desperately hunting for that damned spy as well. I thought if I could bring Gail here in a low profile role, he might get me some leads on who it might be.' Laran leaned back in his chair and fixed his intense, dark emerald eyes on Lilly. She felt herself blushing and cleared her throat.

'Althea, do you think we can trust him?' Lilly asked telepathically.

'Who else is there? We have to get some help from one of them.'

'I want to trust him, but there's something holding me back. Something about him makes me feel uncomfortable, as though he's hiding something from me.'

'You need to read your mother's file and stop listening to all the gossip about him.'

'I know it's odd that Gran never talked about him. The mere mention of him seems to upset her.'

'Read the file.'

Lilly sat up straight and took a deep breath.

'Laran, I don't know if you've heard, but I've been having a bit of trouble lately with Taranis.' Lilly collected her thoughts.

'Trust him, Lilly. He told us about Gail; he could have denied everything,' Althea said telepathically.

'Laran,' Lilly paused as there was a knock on the door and Gail walked in. Laran glanced at the clock on the wall. It was past twelve.

'Sorry Dad, I can come back later,' Gail apologised.

'No, Gail. It's fine. Why don't we all go to lunch together? Get away from the office.'

'Yes, that would be perfect.' Lilly smiled for the first time in their conversation.

'Althea, you'd better change if we're going outside,' Lilly reminded Althea.

'Oh yeah!' Althea quickly nipped into the ladies' room and emerged two minutes later looking like a young, twenty-year-old woman, perfectly dressed for the office. The only thing that showed that she was still Althea was her long, purple hair.

'Better?' Althea winked, making Lilly chuckle as they made their way towards Laran and Gail at the lifts.

'You're making the right decision, Lilly,' Althea said telepathically.

'Perhaps if we share this information, we can solve this mess and bring Taranis back in line.'

'Okay Dad, what's going on?' Gail asked under his breath as the two of them walked toward the lift.

'Not sure really, but I think it has something to do with the children being at the castle the other week.'

'Oh, what makes you think that?'

'Just a hunch,' Laran said quickly as the two women came towards them.

Gail did a double take at Althea, who smirked and gazed up at him through her lashes.

'Althea, you look great,' Gail managed. 'I knew Guardian Elves could morph their appearance, but I've never seen it before.' He swallowed and moved his feet nervously as Althea took his hand. Lilly and Laran tried not to laugh.

'Behave Al,' Lilly warned Althea telepathically.

'Aw, I'm just having a little fun! He's cute.'

Laran took them to a small Italian restaurant near to the FERA offices. Once they were all seated and had ordered, Laran looked at Lilly inquisitively.

'You mentioned you were having trouble with my brother, Taranis. Is it something I can help you with?' Laran smiled, hoping to reassure Lilly. She still seemed jumpy.

'Yes... I have.' Lilly paused as the waiter brought over their drinks.

'Go on,' Laran invited, sensing her indecision. 'I had heard something about the children being in the castle, but not the circumstances behind their visit,' Laran said. 'I assumed they were there by invitation since you and Queen Winter are on such friendly terms.'

'Oh, yes, we are. But this incident had nothing to do with Queen Winter.'

'Oh?' Laran raised a brow.

'It's a long story.' Laughing nervously, Lilly smoothed her skirt. 'Well,' she started, 'When the children were in King Winter's castle, well they, and I know it's illegal and they shouldn't have done it but…' Lilly stopped babbling and took a deep breath and spoke all at once. 'They got this from Taranis's computer!' She held out the memory stick and placed it on the white tablecloth before her.

Gail glanced at it and then glanced at his dad before picking up his glass and sipping his water. Laran picked up the device and looked at it.

'What's on it?' he asked, slipping it into his pocket.

'His accounts, emails, all sorts. I only got a brief look at it myself, but it seemed pretty bad.'

'What kind of bad?' Laran asked.

'I'm not certain, but I think he's been trying to buy the favour of the Dark Elves. He also has a file on me and my family. He was after Willow. I don't know why. The Elder Council is supposed to protect her, not put her in harm's way. I suspect he took her to get at me. But I don't know why.'

'Have you shown it to anyone else?' Laran asked.

'Only Lord Hurleston knows I have it and he hasn't seen what's on it,' Lilly said, trying to read the expression on Laran's face.

'I see.' Laran paused, inspecting his lunch. 'You took a risk showing this to me. How do you know I'm not in with Taranis?' he asked, eventually.

'I don't…'

Laran smiled as he sipped his wine. 'Well, luckily for you, I'm not. In fact, I've been wondering what he's been up to myself. Lord Hurleston already has people keeping tabs on Taranis, but that's probably as far as he's willing to take things. I'll tell you what, I'll talk to some of my people and make sure we have enough muscle to put some serious pressure on Taranis. That should convince him to think twice before doing anything rash.'

'So, I can trust you?' said Lilly, her voice wavering. She cleared her throat and strengthened her voice. 'And you would work with me on this?'

'Yes, you can trust us. Do you mind if Gail helps me with this? I think that would be better than involving anyone else in the department.

And Lilly, whoever Taranis is working with, they might try to kidnap the children again. They will be more aggressive next time,' he warned.

'I'll bear that in mind.'

Gail walked along the street back to FERA, waiting for his father to speak.

'So, the children didn't have an accident. They were kidnapped.' Laran pursed his lips, focusing on the pavement ahead.

'Why would Taranis do that?' Gail asked, frowning slightly. 'Dad, do you think I'm still safe here? Maybe I should go home, back to Canada.'

'What makes you say that?' Laran raised a brow, surprised by Gail's suggestion.

'I don't know. But if the children's misadventure was Taranis trying to gain leverage against Lilly, what's stopping him from using me against you?' Gail frowned as he rubbed his chin while thinking.

'You're safe Gail. This is to do with Lilly, not me,' Laran reassured Gail. 'Taranis really underestimated them. Smart kids. They escaped — but not before copying some of his files.'

Laran laughed and the beginnings of a smile touched Gail's lips.

'Yeah, wish I could have seen Taranis's face when he found out what they'd done.'

'Young Willow will be a force to be reckoned with when she becomes Mother Nature. I hear she's a bright little thing and a bit of a handful.'

'Not so vulnerable, then?' Gail retorted. 'Perhaps we will find something good on the memory stick, like files labelled 'Top Secret' or 'Do Not Let FERA Agents Read'?'

'I will have a proper look. Hopefully it will reveal what Taranis is up to. Kidnapping isn't really his style – and Solstice will be livid. She's quite close to Lilly. I suspect someone else is pulling the strings.' Laran paused. 'I also think those children are far from safe.'

'What do you suggest we do?' said Gail, as they entered the FERA building.

'At the moment, nothing. We look through these files to find out what exactly Taranis is up to – and perhaps who really is behind all this...' Laran trailed off, deep in thought. 'Oh, and Gail – I want you close. Don't go anywhere without telling me, okay? Just to be safe.'

'Yeah, if you say so – although, I can take care of myself in a scrap, Dad.'

'I'm sure you can, but there's no point causing undue worry now, is there? I will send you the files; I want you to go through them really thoroughly, alright?' Laran stepped into the lift with Gail.

'Yeah, thanks Dad,' Gail replied dryly. Visions of boredom stretched before him.

'But Dad, Mother Nature's Elf, she knew my name.' Gail looked at his dad searchingly.

'It's fine Gail, you're still safe. You can trust her. Though she was outrageously flirting with you. I might have a word with her about that,' Laran laughed.

Gail chuckled in agreement. 'It's amazing how she can change her appearance like that. Did she know my birth mother?'

'No, I don't think so, although her predecessor did, Holly's Guardian Elf.' Laran looked at Gail. 'Sorry Gail, there is next to no information about your mother.'

Gail smiled. 'It's okay, Dad. I know. I looked when I was at university.' They stepped out of the lift together.

'Right, clear your desk and then meet me in my office in, say, half an hour? I will let everyone know you're just working with me from now on.'

'Right, okay... So what are we doing?' Gail asked hesitantly, chewing his bottom lip.

'We're going to have a look at this memory stick.'

CHAPTER THREE

Willow flipped through her herbal remedies book in her Gran's study. William had stopped sulking and was upstairs with Heli and Tammy, busy with his new games console.

'Okay, Willow, what's bothering you?' Rose asked, studying her granddaughter.

'If I tell you, you won't laugh, will you?' Willow smiled weakly as she sat in the empty chair by the window, watching the rabbits dance about on the lawn.

'No, of course not. Now come on, what's up?' said Rose.

'If I concentrate, I can hear what the rabbits are saying,' Willow said at last. 'Although they don't speak – not like you and me, but I can hear them in my head.' Willow took a deep breath. 'It started a few weeks ago. I was sitting in our garden, and I realised I could hear the insects. At first it was indistinct, but the more I concentrated, the more I understood what they were saying.' Willow gazed out the window again. 'At first, I didn't mind. It was fun. Then weird stuff happened, and I got scared. That's why I was coming to see you the other day…' Willow fell silent again.

Rose waited, sensing there was more.

'Gran, is there something wrong with me? Was what happened at the tree my fault? If it was, I didn't mean to hurt William – and what if I hurt him again? Or Jacen? What if I hurt Jacen?' Willow blurted out, looking at Rose distressfully.

Rose smiled warmly. 'Is that what's been bothering you?'

Willow nodded her head sadly. The innocence on her face reminded Rose of when she was just a child.

'Let me tell you something that perhaps your mother and I should have told you sooner. My darling, you've been born into a very special family and as you get older, you will develop some very special talents. Don't be frightened, accept them. The tree wasn't your fault, and you won't ever hurt anybody.'

'You mean Mum can hear them too?' Willow asked in disbelief.

'Yes darling, she can. Have you never thought it odd that we have Elves?' replied Rose.

'Well, sort of. I just assumed other people had them too, but just didn't advertise it. After all, I'm supposed to keep Heli a secret. I know only a few people can see the Elves, you know, like Jacen. And obviously his mum because she's been friends with Mum forever.'

'Yes, Sarah is a very special person. Other people have Elves – but not many. They're there to protect you. And the talents you're developing are why you need them. But like the Elves, you must be very careful to whom you show these talents. There are people who might try to harm you or make you do things that might harm others.'

'Oh Gran, I will be careful.' Willow jumped out of her chair to give her grandmother a hug. 'I thought I was going mad, you know!'

'No, my darling. You are simply the Child of Nature. It's a great honour. Enjoy it.'

'But what does that mean? What is a Child of Nature?'

'It's just a formal title given to the successor of Mother Nature.'

'So, one day I'm going to be Mother Nature?' Willow asked. 'What does that even mean? What does Mum actually do?'

'Your mother is a very important person, who does environmental work for the government. There'll be a time when you'll need to know what exactly, and your mother and I will be here to help you make the transition. But until then, you don't need to worry too much, darling. For now, just you concentrate on being young and having a good time,' she said before giving Willow a gentle hug.

★★★★

Laran was trawling through Taranis's accounts when a knock at the door interrupted him. He stood up and was surprised to see Solstice. She wore a smart white dress with a black belt that matched her heels.

'Hello Laran, do you have a minute?' she asked.

'Yes, of course – come right in, what brings you to FERA?' Laran replied, giving her a smile and pulling out a chair out for her.

'Thank you. I'm having lunch with Lilly today,' Solstice said as she sat down.

'So, what did you want to discuss? Has Taranis done something?'

'Not that I'm aware of. I was actually here to talk about you.'

'Oh, really?' Laran replied, his voice low and husky. It had the desired effect, coaxing Solstice into smiling back as she ran her tongue over her bottom lip. 'What about me had you come to discuss exactly?' He was wondering how far this would go. They had had dalliances in the past. He wondered if that was what this was about.

'Actually, it's about Lilly,' Solstice said.

'Oh.'

'I know you've been helping her lately, which I appreciate.' Solstice reached for his hand on the desk and took a breath. 'It's just, well, I think you need to step back a bit.'

'I'm not sure I understand. Are you telling me to back off?' Laran opened his mouth and shut it again.

'Yes Laran, I am,' Solstice sighed. 'Lilly's not her mother. I know she looks just like Holly, but that's probably where the similarities end. Lilly is completely different. She's kind and trusting, and her responsibilities and priorities differ completely from Holly's. What's more, she is certainly not used to men like you.' Solstice hoped she didn't sound too harsh.

'Yes, I know Lilly isn't Holly. I loved Holly. I obviously don't have those feelings for Lilly. But I don't really think any of this is your concern,' Laran spoke sharply.

'Yes, it is my concern,' said Solstice. 'It concerns us all. I don't want you to get hurt. How does Annie feel about you spending so much time with Lilly?'

Laran pulled his hand away and glared at Solstice. 'Annie trusts how I spend my time. Besides, we aren't exactly alone when working.' Laran folded his arms across his chest.

Solstice continued, 'We can't lose another Mother Nature. Not after last time. That not only nearly destroyed the Elder Council, but it also nearly destroyed you. Please Laran, try to remember that this is Lilly: delicate, fragile Lilly, and unlike Holly, she can't go charging after you into battle and end up getting mixed up in one of your endless wars – accidentally or otherwise.'

Laran's face flushed bright red in anger. 'Rose put you up to this, didn't she? You can tell her I'm not trying to get Lilly mixed up in any wars. I'm just trying to help her bring your husband back into line. What did Taranis think he was doing, kidnapping the children like that? We are supposed to protect the Child of Nature – not deliberately put her in harm's way. Where were you when all this was going on?'

'How dare you!' Solstice exclaimed. 'I don't control him. I came here hoping I could talk some sense into you and help prevent things from turning out the way they did last time – after all, it was you that got burnt the most, wasn't it?' Solstice argued icily before getting up to leave the room.

Laran jumped to his feet. 'Solstice, wait!' She stopped before opening the door.

'You're right,' he sighed, massaging his temples. 'I'm sorry. Maybe I should distance myself from Lilly. But you and I are the only ones she can rely on for help with this. I know you don't

47

like to admit it, but Taranis is working against her and now I've got evidence that Hyperion's involved as well. The Springs don't like to get involved, Queen Andarta and I don't talk, and Queen Alectrona is busy organising the Summer Elves. There's no one else for her to talk to.'

'Well, I suppose you're correct,' Solstice said.

'I know you're looking out for me, and I am grateful for that, but you don't need to worry about Lilly and me. I would be indebted to you if you could talk to Taranis. This isn't like him. Find out what's going on.'

'Why don't you go to Alectrona? If Hyperion really is involved, we may need Alectrona's help to stop him, anyway. See if you can convince her to help. And I'll speak to Taranis.'

★★★★

Lilly sat on the sofa in the small flat, gifted to her by FERA for when she had to work in London for long periods of time. In her lap lay a small manila folder with her mother's name written on top. Lilly ran her fingers over it and briefly closed her eyes. She took a deep breath and removed the crumpled sheets of paper from inside.

Post Action Report: Operation Death Stroke
Classification: Top Secret

On 5th of November 1987, the Summer Fifth Army captured the Dark Elf Stronghold of Izhevsk. Among those captured was a Dark Elf General, who claimed that he knew the location of the Dark Elf Emperor. In return for his life and freedom, he promised to give us the Emperor's location.

He claimed the Dark Elf High Command was holed up in a French fortress town.

Having successfully engaged and defeated a Dark Elf force in northern Romania, I immediately consulted Mother Nature on our next movements. She agreed that a surgical strike to wipe out the leaders of the Dark Elf Army was the best course of action. I immediately redeployed the Autumn Elf First Army to France.

Upon arrival, the Spring Army was already in the French theatre of war, led by King and Queen Spring. Queen Spring had since attacked a Dark Elf force twenty miles north of the Emperor's supposed coordinates. This was a strategic error: the Emperor certainly would have known we were coming by the time Mother Nature and I arrived in France. We quickly surrounded the Emperor's fortress and began laying siege to it. It soon became apparent they had a sizable garrison of elite forces; however, his closest reinforcements were fighting Queen Spring in the north. After Queen Summer's victory over the Dark Elf Second Army in Russia, the Emperor would have known no help was on its way.

Mother Nature, General Aristata, and I devised a plan to storm the fortress.

King Spring was going to attack the gate with his Spring forces. General Aristata would support them. Meanwhile, Mother Nature and I would lead the troops over the walls in a surprise attack against the soldiers defending the gate. Then we would proceed along the main boulevard toward the fortress, fight our way in and capture – or kill – the Dark Elf Emperor and his closest advisors.

The first part of the plan went well: while King Spring and General Aristata led the attack on the gate, myself, Mother Nature, and ten of my best soldiers used grappling hooks to scale the walls to launch a surprise attack. The Dark Elves were quickly defeated. We battled our way along the wall and captured the gatehouse with little resistance. We opened the main gate for King Spring and many of our forces flooded into the fortress. But soon, the Dark Elves quickly recovered from their original panic and fought back. After intense combat, the Dark Elf forces wavered and retreated towards the fortress. My troops, sensing their advantage, rushed after them, and funnelled into a large courtyard directly in front of the fortress. I quickly found Mother Nature and ensured she stayed out of the courtyard with me. Something didn't feel right.

I realised my fears when the gate to the courtyard slammed down, cleaving a Spring Elf in half, and trapping King Spring and a hundred Spring and Autumn warriors inside. Then machine guns opened fire on them, massacring them. King Spring fell alongside his men.

Meanwhile, Mother Nature and I found a small postern gate, which led into the fortress. We fought our way in and managed to get behind the machine gun emplacements, killing their operators. But a large portion of our force was already destroyed, and the rest of our Elves were weakening against the tenacious defence of the Dark Elves.

If it hadn't been for Queen Summer and her army's timely arrival, we would have lost the battle. She led a brilliant counter-attack into the empty courtyard, smashing down the gate to the fortress and rushing inside with her troops. Mother Nature and I pushed deeper into the fortress, looking for the Emperor and the throne room.

As we were making our way through the inner passages of the fortress, a group of the

Emperor's Elite Guard jumped us. Mother Nature and I were separated. She proceeded deeper into the fortress, looking for the Emperor. I found Queen Summer and her troops in the entrance hall.

As I crossed the entrance hall towards the throne home, she advised, 'Don't kill them all instantly. I want them alive.'

'Why? After this, we've won. It'll all be over.'

'Some of them have been of use to me, and in return I promised to spare their lives,' she replied as we entered the throne room.

Everyone was already dead. The Emperor was slumped over his throne and drenched in blood — his throat had been slit.

'Have your men already been here?' Queen Summer demanded.

'Not that I know of,' I replied.

'Then he betrayed me,' Queen Summer replied.

'Who betrayed you?' I asked as General Aristata walked in, followed by his few remaining men.

'What happened?' he asked.

'It wasn't us.'

'Oh, well, most of the Dark Elves are retreating, dead or have surrendered.'

'Great. Have you seen Mother Nature?'

'No, I didn't. Wasn't she with you?'

'We got separated.'

'He's not here. Mother Nature's in danger. Come on,' Queen Summer urged as she stormed out of the room.

'Who's not here? What aren't you telling me?' I demanded, following her.

We found no sign of this mysterious associate of Queen Summer's. We did, however, recover Mother Nature's body. She had been killed. We sadly could not identify her killer.

Thus concludes my report on Operation Death Stroke. The operation was a success, but came at the significant cost of Mother Nature's life.

Signed,
Laran, King Autumn and Commander-in-Chief of the Autumn Army.

It was a cold, clinical report. Lilly looked inside the folder and then, there in the middle, she saw an envelope with her name written on it. With shaking hands, Lilly opened it.

Dear Lilly,

I feel compelled to write this to you so that one day you will understand. If you are reading this, you must be Mother Nature, and I must be dead.

It broke my heart to see you holding your father's hand, tears running down your cheeks as we waited for the train that would take you from me forever.

Please never doubt that I love you. For years now, I have been two people, and I have realised that I must choose.

Please don't hate me. Maybe one day when you have a daughter, you will understand.

Lilly shut her eyes. She remembered that day. How she had said goodbye to her mother, not really understanding why they had to be separated.

Then something else floated up through Lilly's subconscious. There had been another man. He had his arm around her mother's waist. Lilly forced the memory into sharper focus. It had been Laran holding her mother as the train pulled out of the station.

Lilly's eyes flew open. That had been the last time Lilly had seen her mother. A week later, Holly would be dead, Laran would be mentally and physically broken, and the Elder Council would almost tear itself apart. Lilly picked up the letter once again.

I truly loved you and your father, and the decision to send you both away was not taken lightly. I knew I might never see you again. Take care of your father. I hope he will move on and understand why with time.

You will be a wonderful Mother Nature. Don't doubt yourself and always trust your gut instinct.

Your ever-loving mother,
Holly

Tears ran freely down her cheeks. Her mother had loved Laran, which ultimately cost her life.

CHAPTER FOUR

The bright sunshine cast a dappled shade around Willow and William and their two Elves as they walked along the lane leading to the village. Gran had sent them to get some fresh air and snacks and they were bickering about how much time William had spent playing on his games console. William fell silent and nodded politely to a passing dog walker with a large Alsatian.

'Willow, that's like the fifth dog walker we've seen since we left Gran's,' William said.

'So?'

'How many people own dogs in this village? Don't you think it's weird?'

'I think you're weird,' Willow replied, without looking up from her phone.

'Ah, forget it,' scoffed William. Willow smiled sweetly and returned to her texting.

William spoke after a brief silence. 'Willow, do you think Suzy will be working today?'

'Dunno. Why?' Willow glanced at William.

'Well, Tom reckons she fancies me.' Willow snorted and went back to texting Jacen as the four of them entered the corner shop.

Moments later, they emerged, carrying an assortment of crisps and chocolate bars. William was beaming from ear to ear as he opened a packet of Starburst.

'I got her number!' he announced.

'So?' Willow said dismissively, causing William's face to fall.

'Really? Are you going to call her then?' Heli asked, linking arms with William.

'Well, yeah. Don't you think I should?' William asked, his voice coated with doubt.

'Of course you should!'

'You know, there are an awful lot of dogs in this village,' William said again, as another dog walker passed them.

Willow grunted in response as she carried on texting.

Meanwhile, Tammy pulled Heli to a halt. 'Heli, those dogs don't feel right to me.' Heli frowned and closed her eyes in concentration.

'Oh no, you're right! That's because they aren't dogs. Oh no! Tammy, the children!' Heli opened her eyes wide, startled at what she had felt. 'Come on, we need to warn them!' Heli took Tammy's hand and ran down the lane after Willow and William.

Willow pushed open the door to Gran's house, while William hung back slightly. He glanced up and down the lane while slowly chewing another sweet. It was unusually empty. William lingered for a moment longer, unable to shake the feeling that something was wrong. Maybe he was just being paranoid.

'Gran?' Willow called out as she stepped inside the house. Confused by the silence, she cautiously walked through the kitchen and gasped when she entered the living room to find Gran tied up on the sofa. A tall, handsome man dressed in a cream suit stood peering at his reflection in the mirror that hung above the fireplace.

William was about to step inside when he saw Heli and Tammy running frantically towards him. Heli stopped in front of him, bending double to get her breath back.

'William,' Heli gasped, 'You were right. The dogs are Dark Elves. Where is Willow? We have to get out of here now!'

'She's inside already!' He grabbed Heli and pulled her onto the porch. 'We're too late,' he thought telepathically as one of the dog walkers they had passed approached them.

'Gran!' Willow shouted and turned to run out the door to warn William, only to find the dog walker from earlier was now holding a jagged black blade to William's throat.

Five other dog walkers stood outside while one dog seemed to stretch and grow; its skin darkened as it morphed before their eyes into a purple-skinned Humanoid with pointed ears. A short black blade appeared in its hand. The Elf had dark hair, red eyes and a row of small, pointed teeth. It towered above them and was powerfully built. It wore some sort of dark brown, layered leather armour that covered its legs and chest. Its large biceps were bare as it pointed its sword towards Tammy and Heli, who were backed into a corner.

'Ah! Hello! You must be Willow. It is a pleasure to meet you at last. I'm King Summer, you may curtsey if you like!' The blond-haired man smiled charmingly at Willow, who scowled back. 'Don't scowl. You're lucky I'm here. Left to their own devices, these naughty chaps would happily kill you. But we wouldn't want to ruin your Gran's lovely rug with blood now, would we? You're going to come with us quietly and without a struggle, or I will hurt your Gran. Understood?'

'What about the boy and the Guardian Elves? We only want her. We should kill them.' The dog walker holding William had now morphed into another Dark Elf.

'No, why must you be so violent all the time? There's something about this boy.' Hyperion stared at William. 'He reminds me of someone, but I can't think who.' William's face was a mask of cold fury, and he balled his hands into fists. Hyperion smiled as if he was enjoying himself.

'I'm sure I'll figure it out eventually. Bring the Elves too. We might need some hostages. Rose, always good to catch up, no hard feelings, I hope,' Hyperion said cheerfully as the intruders marched out of the house.

Holding onto their hostages, the Dark Elves walked into the shadow cast by the house. In a flash, they all vanished and just as suddenly, they stood in the dark shadows of King Winter's castle.

It had changed dramatically since they were last there. Snow was falling heavily, reaching their knees now, and security guards were nowhere to be seen. These looming creatures, which appeared to be made entirely of ice, had replaced them. Others resembled terrifying snowmen with long white fur, sharp teeth, and claws.

Taranis stood in the hall and watched silently as the group entered his home. His face was expressionless, but Willow immediately knew that the Winter King wasn't happy.

'These are prisoners, not guests,' Hyperion announced. 'I'm throwing them into the dungeon. And you will not tell Queen Winter of their presence. Do you understand?' Hyperion instructed Taranis.

'Yes, I understand. Get them out of here,' Taranis replied miserably.

'And stop sulking. I want this damned snow to stop. I hate the cold.'

Taranis ignored him. *This was so wrong*, he told himself. Last time, Mother Nature had let the incident go as the children hadn't been harmed, but she wouldn't be so forgiving this time. He had also heard she was now working with Laran. This was all getting out of hand, especially now Hyperion had brought Dark Elves into his castle.

'Our mother will find out about this. When she gets here, she'll be mad as hell!' Willow shouted. When she received no response, she cried desperately, 'You can stop this! You can let us go now and we'll forget this ever happened!'

William was trying to signal something to Taranis. Taranis stared at him blankly. Although he didn't understand sign language, he assumed whatever William was trying to say wasn't for the faint of heart.

He turned his back on the scene, trudging back to his office. Taranis could only dread what was to come. He was sick of King Summer. *Let Mother Nature come*, he thought to himself bitterly. Although if she was bringing Laran with her, he was going to need the support of all four of the Winter Lords to have any sort of hope against his army.

He immediately ordered a council meeting at the castle and, merely an hour later, the Winter Lords arrived with their confidants.

Lord Boreas was first to arrive and upon entering the great hall, he and his retinue bowed deeply. 'My King, what may I ask is the purpose of this impromptu gathering?' he asked, doing little to disguise his bemusement at Taranis' antics.

'I shall inform you all the reasons for this meeting, once everyone is present. How are things in the north?'

'The northern lands are not faring well, my King. Every summer, more and more of the pack ice is eroded, and every winter, less and less is replenished. Your northernmost kingdoms have almost halved in size, and if the Humans continue, they might disappear completely,' Lord Boreas replied, his expression grim.

At that moment, Lord Auster and Lord Aquillo arrived.

'Lord Auster, Lord Aquillo, I thank you for coming with such haste. Please accompany us to the dining room, where we shall wait for Lord Septentrio.'

'Septentrio sends his apologies. He has been working with the Humans on some mining operation but assured me he would get here as soon as he can,' Lord Aquillo explained.

'I hear you and Septentrio have been working on this project together.'

'Yes sir, but I am merely handling the finances and logistics. Septentrio is the mining engineer,' Aquillo answered.

Not much longer later, Lord Septentrio entered the room with his attendant, both still dressed for the Arctic. Although the cold didn't bother Winter Elves, they wore clothes to blend in with the Humans.

'I apologise for my late arrival, my King,' Septentrio bowed, before removing his coat.

'Now that we are all settled. Let me explain why I have called you here at such short notice. Gentlemen, the Winter Kingdom is under attack. We are, as of this moment, at war,' Taranis announced grimly.

'War?' Lord Auster asked in disbelief.

'How can this be?' Lord Septentrio demanded. 'I have just come from our most northern territory.'

'How is this the first we have heard of this?' Lord Boreas asked.

'Who exactly are we at war with? The Dark Elves again?' Lord Aquillo asked sceptically. He was the most practical of the lords.

'No, we are at war with the Humans,' Taranis replied.

'The Humans? You must be joking, Mother Nature forbade even revealing our existence to them, let alone going to war with them,' Lord Boreas exclaimed, confusion and anger fusing together on his face.

'Lord Boreas is right. The other immortals will never allow it. Besides, I have been working closely with the Humans. I would have felt some sort of tension if what you say is true.' Lord Septentrio frowned.

'What is there to gain in going to war with the Humans?' Lord Boreas spluttered.

'And the Humans vastly outnumber us, let alone the fact they're better armed. We could never defeat them,' Lord Aquillo added.

Taranis was angry now. 'Every year, our kingdom gets smaller and smaller due to their recklessness. Their cars and their fossil fuels are ruining this planet! I'm sick of paying for their foolishness, having to watch my territories melt away while they blunder around in their ignorance! Enough is enough! Plus, we won't be engaging the Humans directly. We'll be making use of our very own super weapon… Mother Nature herself.'

'My King, Mother Nature would never help us against the Humans,' said Lord Boreas, while some of the other lords nodded in agreement.

'She will if she has no other choice. If we blackmail her,' King Winter declared.

'My King, how do you intend to blackmail her?' Lord Septentrio asked.

'Her children, of course,' he announced. His earlier doubt had now transformed into defiant confidence.

'You intend to kidnap her children, my King?' Lord Auster asked in disbelief.

'Well, we've already kidnapped them.'

'What? Have you gone completely mad?' Lord Boreas exploded.

'Calm down, Boreas. King Winter must know what he is doing,' Lord Aquillo interjected. 'However, you must realise, my King, that Mother Nature will not be bullied. When she learns of this, she will come for her children, and I doubt she will come alone,' he continued as Lord Septentrio and Aquillo murmured in agreement.

'As powerful as Mother Nature is, the Dark Elves are stronger in battle. I'm more afraid of her alliance with King Autumn. The Autumn Elves are formidable warriors and will put up a strong fight. I will need your armies to make this work. If we succeed, we can repair the Human damage done to this world before it's too late,' King Winter argued emphatically.

The Winter Lords sat in an eerie silence before Lord Boreas rose to his feet. He placed his right hand on his chest and proclaimed, 'I have pledged my allegiance to you, my King. I intend to honour that oath; you shall have my troops.'

Just as he had finished speaking, Lord Auster stood up and pledged his allegiance.

Lord Septentrio, however, was not so certain. 'Hold on. I know Willow and William, and I cannot and will not condone using them in this way. You are vastly underestimating Mother Nature. She will not take this lightly and I, for one, do not want to make an enemy of her. I understand your anger with the Humans, but this is not the way forward. Show me a better way and you can have my army.' The young Lord stared defiantly at his King as the other Lords looked on in shock.

'I respect your decision, and I cannot force you,' Taranis answered. 'You are dismissed. I only ask you do not publicly go against me.'

'You will always have my loyalty,' Lord Septentrio answered, rising from his chair and bowing to his King before leaving.

'And you, Lord Aquillo?' Taranis raised a brow as he surveyed the youngest and least experienced Lord.

'I will help you in any way I can, but like Lord Septentrio, I worry about using the children. I've also heard the rumours that Mother Nature's working with King Autumn. His son has returned fully trained by Hàlfr; I don't fancy going up against him. Even without Lord Septentrio, we outnumber the Autumn Army by about twenty thousand. My men aren't the best fighters, but they are excellent strategists.'

'Excellent, I guarantee I shall reward you once we win this war. Now make the arrangements. We must be ready to defend this castle immediately,' Taranis ordered.

'Yes, my King,' the three Lords echoed as one, as they silently dispersed from the dining hall.

Only a few hours later, the armies arrived. Taranis was feeling confident they could hold off an attack from Laran and his Autumn Army. He entered the castle through the side door to avoid Hyperion and his Dark Elves.

'I hate those bloody Dark Elves,' he muttered to himself as he pushed his office door open to find Solstice pacing the length of the room.

'Solstice, what are you doing here?' he said, surprised as he slumped himself into his large padded chair.

'I live here, Taranis. Why shouldn't I be here?' Solstice retorted. She waited for him to reply and when he didn't, she marched over to his chair and brought her face inches from his.

'You've ruined my rose garden! It was one of the best in Europe, did you know? Of course not! Because you spend all your time running around with that stupid Hyperion. I've won the Chelsea flower show five times, Taranis! Alan Titchmarsh said I have a gift. And you've gone and ruined it with all this ruddy snow!' Solstice snapped.

'Go and live with Alan Titchmarsh then, if you value his opinion so much,' Taranis shot back, feeling his mood go from bad to worse. He gazed longingly at his drinks cabinet, wishing Solstice would leave him in peace.

'Why are you doing this?' Solstice asked. 'I don't understand! Why do you think going along with Hyperion's schemes will make things any better for us?' Solstice asked, trying to control her temper.

'Why am I doing this? Why do you think?' Taranis exclaimed. 'I'm sick of being the third wheel – the quiet, boring one nobody cares about or listens to.'

Solstice looked at him in disbelief. 'What are you talking about, Taranis? Are you hearing yourself?' Solstice said. 'That's completely ridiculous. What are you so jealous of?'

'God, it rattles me that everyone's scared of Laran. I hate that they respect his opinion more than mine, and Mother Nature only seems to care what he has to say. Why does she prefer him over me? He's the reason her mother's dead. I used to be consulted by everyone, revered and respected. Now it's all about bloody Laran.'

'This is ludicrous, Taranis. People do respect your opinion, and you're just as powerful as Laran. But if you spend all your time hiding away in this castle, playing the gentleman farmer, she won't care what you have to say, will she?' Solstice huffed. 'When was the last time you went to the office? Or offered to help? She talks to Laran because he's there. Because he takes an active interest in her life and her job. He's not here, hiding away.'

Taranis stood up and walked to the drinks cabinet as a stony silence stretched between them. Solstice watched as he angrily unscrewed the lid of a bottle of scotch and poured it into a glass, splashing it onto the surface. He took a long gulp and slammed the glass back down.

'I don't like the way you keep talking to me, Solstice. Of all people, you should show me a little more respect.' Taranis turned around to face her. 'I hardly even see you anymore. Even you spend more time with Laran than you do with me.' Taranis poured himself another scotch.

Solstice opened her mouth to retaliate, but nothing seemed to come out. The wind howled and beat at the windowpane as snow fell heavier than ever outside.

'You know what? Forget it. I can't deal with this right now,' Taranis turned away from her, finished his drink and stormed out of his office, slamming the door behind him.

Solstice stood helpless, frozen with rage, as tears cascaded down her cheeks. She picked up his empty glass and threw it at the door, letting out a sob as she watched it shatter into pieces across the floor.

★★★★

Gail stood in Laran's office, peering over his shoulder at the computer screen. 'These accounts are so cluttered. It's as if he was trying to make them deliberately complicated.'

'I agree. I've been trawling through King Winter's accounts all morning. He's got dummy corporations and false bank accounts set up everywhere,' Laran muttered in response.

'And he kept track of it all on this one computer?'

'Apparently so. Lilly's kids have got it all. Gail, I need you to investigate this thoroughly, alright?'

Gail sighed dramatically. 'If you say so,' he agreed reluctantly, before taking the memory stick and walking back to his office.

Four hours later, Laran's hunch was proven correct: Taranis and Hyperion had been buying exclusively into building companies and real estate agents. They had also been buying up seemingly unrelated plots of land, many of which appeared to be useless.

Gail picked up his phone and dialled his dad's internal number. 'Dad, can you send me all FERA's files on Hyperion's and Taranis's real estate investments?' He then emailed the head of FERA's Department of Intelligence and organised a meeting.

The FERA Department of Intelligence was located just one floor down, so Gail didn't have far to go.

'Enter,' the Director of Intelligence, Markus Kendrick, called after Gail knocked politely on the door. Markus was tall and slender, dressed sharply in an expensive grey suit.

'Have a seat. How can I help you, Prince Autumn?'

'Actually, it's just Gail. I'm not royalty,' Gail replied.

'Understood.'

'Sir, I've been doing some research into King Summer and King Winter's real estate interests, and I've discovered that Taranis and Hyperion have been buying land previously belonging to the Dark Elves. Sometimes, even going as far as deliberately stalling Human construction projects that would intrude into Dark Elf territory.'

'How have you come by this information?' Kendrick asked, raising an eyebrow.

'My father passed me some files, sir. It's part of a project he is working on with Mother Nature.'

'I see. Will I be able to view these files you speak of?' Kendrick smiled, knowing he was making the boy nervous.

'Yes, sir. We will pass them on to your department in due course. Would it be possible for you to send me any information that might confirm my suspicions? Just any information regarding any known Dark Elf properties and strongholds or known Dark Elf sympathisers within the other Elven houses. As well as any other intel along those lines so I can cross-reference the information.' Gail quickly added, 'Please?'

'I'll put someone on it straightaway.'

Gail offered his gratitude to Markus and quickly returned to his own office. He glanced at the clock on the wall; it was five thirty already — he was meeting his father in half an hour. Gail smiled as he stretched out the kinks in his back, excited at the opportunity to tell his father about the land Taranis had been buying up. However, a sudden flash of anger surged through him, followed by paralysing fear. Frowning to himself, Gail stood up to shut his window and reached for his blazer. It was a mild evening in August. Why were his arms suddenly covered in goosebumps?

It suddenly dawned on Gail that these random feelings weren't his but William's, which were coming to him through the link they shared. But why would William be cold when it was the hottest August since records began? *I need to find my dad and quick*, he thought to himself, as he shut the link and desperately tried to block out the feelings.

'Dad, I think the children are in trouble,' Gail said, shuddering as he barged into his dad's office.

'What makes you think that?' Laran frowned. 'Are you alright?'

'No, I'm cold. Really cold. I think it's coming from William, even though I've shut the link. I need to go home now.' Gail's teeth were chattering as he spoke.

'We better get you out of here before someone notices and starts asking questions. Here, take this.' Laran took his coat and handed it to Gail.

'W-w-where are w-we going?' Gail shivered.

'Back to the flat,' Laran replied. 'We need to put you in some warm clothes and get some soup in you. That should warm you up a bit.'

At the flat, Gail sat huddled on the sofa with his duvet wrapped tightly around him. His hands were cupped around a mug of chicken soup and his eyelids drooped as he dozed in and out of sleep.

Suddenly, the doorbell rang, interrupting the quiet hum of the radio in the background. Laran strode over and cautiously opened the door, only to be confronted with a pistol just as it went off. Laran dodged and slammed the arm of the man holding the gun against the doorframe. The intruder was a Dark Elf. The gun fired again, smashing a chunk of plaster out of the wall. Laran elbowed the Elf in the throat, wrestling the pistol out of his wrist. But before Laran could use it himself, the Elf barrelled through the door, knocking him off his feet. The intruder and two other Elves barged past Laran into the threshold.

Meanwhile, Gail frantically tried to get to his feet, tripping over the duvet wrapped around him. Two of the Elves lunged at him as he threw a bowl of scalding soup in their faces. As he made for the kitchen, Laran scrambled to his feet in the hallway and shoved the first Elf face-first against the wall. One of the other Dark Elves, its face blistered by soup, grabbed Laran from behind and pulled. He did not resist and threw his weight backwards; the momentum slammed the maimed Dark Elf into the opposite wall.

In the kitchen, Gail quickly retrieved a knife off the counter and brandished it at the Elf coming towards him. The Dark Elf sneered and flicked out the light. Gail lunged, but the darkness threw his equilibrium into disarray. The Dark Elves had better night vision than him. Gail felt a powerful pair of hands force the knife away from his hand, punching him in the side of his head. Stars exploded before his eyes. In his dazed state, Gail barely noticed the Dark Elf drag him into the shadows.

★★★★

Willow and William sat huddled together in a dark corner of the dungeon, trying to keep each other warm. The walls were covered with ice and hay blackened with dirt covered the floor.

'William? Can you hear me?' Willow tried to ask William telepathically. She hoped their Elves had been taken somewhere better than here. She tapped him on the shoulder and signed to him, asking if he was okay. He signed angrily that he refused to spend any more of his time with her if they were going to get kidnapped every five-flipping-minutes. A moment later, he added he was freezing.

'I'm sorry,' Willow signed back before bursting into tears. William was caught off-guard, and he put his arms around her, regretting that he had been so harsh with her. After all, it wasn't really her fault they were trapped in this awful dungeon. When her tears finally subsided, Willow got up to look around. They needed to get out of there before they froze to death. She started jumping up and down to keep warm.

'Are you alright?' William signed to Willow. She nodded and walked around the

perimeter of the cell. She could feel fear...
Perhaps it was coming from Heli.

Suddenly, she heard footsteps — someone was coming. She grabbed William's arm, pulling him into the darkness of the cell. Two Dark Elves dragged a semi-conscious figure behind them as they stood hidden in the shadows. They dropped the boy to the floor, causing him to groan in pain. They both cackled as they slammed the door shut behind them.

Willow rushed over to the crumpled figure on the ground, gently helping him sit up. A large, purple bruise was forming on the right side of his face.

'Are you alright?' Willow asked worriedly. She felt her cheeks flush as the boy looked back at her.

'I'm good, thanks,' Gail muttered as he struggled to his feet. A wave of dizziness washed over him, and he felt the girl grab him.

'Clearly not. Sit down.' Willow's brow furrowed with concern.

'I'm fine, really, just got up too quickly.' He winced as he touched the bruise on the side of his head.

'I'm Willow. This is my brother, William.'

'I'm Gail. Gail Autumn.'

'I can hear!' William suddenly exclaimed. 'I can hear what you're both saying!'

'Oh! The Elves must be nearby! Maybe Gail saw them.' Willow and William looked at Gail expectantly, who stared back at them blankly. 'Two girls? No older than ten?' Willow continued.

'All the cells I saw were empty. I think we're the only ones here,' Gail replied.

'Oh,' William murmured.

'Why?' Gail asked, obviously confused.

'It doesn't matter,' Willow replied quickly. 'Why are you here? I mean, who are you really?' Willow asked, hoping she didn't sound too rude.

'I'm King Autumn's son,' Gail replied while he examined the metal bars that made up the door, none of which seemed to be old or rusty. He suspected this was just for show and judging by the stack of barrels he could see, and the smell, the dungeon was used to store the estate whiskey.

Willow furrowed her brow thoughtfully. 'We're Mother Nature's children. There must be a reason we're all here together. Maybe King Winter is using us.'

'Yeah, all the other times I have been here I have had a proper bedroom,' Gail chuckled.

'Wow! I have never met a real prince before,' Willow smiled as she watched him rattle the bars on the door.

'I'm not a prince, sorry to disappoint,' Gail said as he ran his hands along the top of the door.

'But how are we going to get out of here?' William moaned through chattering teeth. His skin was turning a bluish colour. In fact, all three of them were looking almost translucent.

'Here, put this on.' Gail passed Willow the cardigan he had put on at his flat.

'Are you sure?' she asked him. He nodded and rubbed his arms with his hands, trying to smile at her.

'What if we made some noise?' She looked at Gail.

'I doubt anyone will hear you. We're in a dungeon.'

Willow started shouting anyway; after all, they would be of no use to King Winter if they froze to death. When they were last here, the place was full of people; she had seen no one this time.

After a while, Willow gave up her futile shouting. Neither Gail nor William had spoken in a while. They sat morosely in opposite corners, barely moving, their eyelids drooping. Willow remembered reading that feeling sleepy was one of the first signs of hypothermia.

'William, Gail, don't go to sleep. You must stay awake!' She ran over to William and wrapped her arms around him, pulling him as close to her as she could. He owed her for this. Big time.

★★★★

Heli wasn't sure where she was exactly. She knew she was in Winter's castle, but she didn't know which room she was in or how to get out. She suspected by the shape of the roof that she was in the attic of one tower, but she had no way of knowing which one. They had tied Tammy up next to her. But Heli couldn't hear her thoughts and had already realised that the Dark Elves were blocking their telepathic powers.

'Tammy, are you alright?' Heli asked. Tammy nodded. 'They are blocking me. I can't talk to Willow or William, and I feel freezing. How are they doing that?' Heli enquired, looking around to see how many Dark Elves were in the room with them.

Tammy finally pulled herself together. 'Dark Elves differ from us,' she explained. 'They have gained unique powers from us because they lived in nasty places and spent so much time practicing their dark, evil magic.' Heli turned away to hide her amusement.

'Okay, that was a little racist,' said Heli, trying to suppress her giggle.

'So, what do we do? Do we have anything that they don't, something to help us get out of here and find Willow and William?' asked Heli, feeling desperate and scared.

'I don't know. I'm working on it. They haven't been a problem in years. I wonder what is upsetting them now. This is not their normal behaviour; they would normally avoid enclosed buildings like this,' Tammy replied.

'I can feel Willow,' remarked Heli. 'Is that any help?'

'No, not really. How is she?' Tammy replied. 'She's really frustrated mostly, and cold.'

'That's not good. Can you remember what they were wearing?' Tammy asked.

'Shorts and T-shirts,' replied Heli.

'We have got to get out of here. They could freeze to death.' Tammy wriggled, trying to loosen her bonds. Heli did the same. The Dark Elves had wandered off, distracted by something outside.

'Not very bright, are they?' Heli remarked. 'Perhaps we could use that to our advantage.'

'Perhaps we can.' Tammy wriggled a bit more and finally her hands came loose. She quickly turned and untied Heli before looking around the room for a way out, or at least for some sort of clue to where they were.

'Thanks,' Heli said, rubbing her wrists. 'Now all we have to do is get Willow and William and get out of this castle.'

'We have to get out of this room first,' Tammy replied. 'If that door is locked, our escape attempt is as good as over.'

'Hey how did you get free?' A massive Dark Elf stomped toward them, making the little Elves shrink back.

'Heli, remember the training I gave you in the garden,' Tammy garbled out quickly as the Elf stood over them.

'Oh yes,' Heli giggled. 'On three.' She glanced at Tammy to see her nod her head. Heli skittered around the Elf and, with a nimble hop, jumped onto his back, rubbing her hands together. She then clamped them on the Elf's head.

'Gerrof,' he stuttered out before his eyes rolled into the back of his head and, with a crash, he toppled over like a felled tree. Heli gracefully jumped off his back and landed in a crouch, turning as two more hulking Dark Elves crashed into the room. 'Well, that solves the door problem,' Heli muttered.

They stopped at the sight of their fallen comrade. Lightning crackled between Heli's hands. Tammy crouched, ready to attack. With a flick of her wrist, blue lightning shot from her fingers and wrapped around one of the Dark Elves, making him scream in pain as he ran from the room, clawing at the electric force that was dancing over his body. He fell down the turret's stairs, causing an almighty ruckus with his shrieks and screams as he bounced down each stone step.

Heli giggled as she turned to see Tammy attack the second Dark Elf, who had been inching closer with deadly intent. Tammy crouched and held her hand up, making a 'come-on' motion. The Elf threw his head back a laughed a deep, guttural laugh before charging at the little Elf.

With the grace of an Olympic gymnast, Tammy vaulted over him, jabbing him with her hand and blasting him off his feet, throwing him against the wall with so much force plaster rained down on his now slumped unconscious form.

Skipping across the room, Tammy took Heli's hand with a giggle as the two small Elves stepped over the defeated Dark Elves and, hand in hand, they exited the room.

'Was that Autumn you channelled?'

'Oh yes, I like the subtlety of it. Can't wait for Willow to get it. William is going to be unconscious a lot,' Heli giggled. 'You still like the dramatic I see.'

'Yep, all the power of Mother Nature without the paperwork,' Tammy answered in a singsong voice while waving her hands in the air.

CHAPTER FIVE

David enjoyed his journeys alone in the car. He could listen to his 'old people's music' with no complaints from the backseat. He hummed along to his playlist, letting his mind wander over his day so far; the beetles he collected last week were being identified and his research into Ash Dieback was showing some results. David thought about the children as he approached Rose's house. His moment of quiet was about to be shattered. They were so noisy and were always arguing. Moody too, especially William. He seemed to be grumpy about anything and everything. Of course, William's moods would be better if Willow didn't spend every waking hour winding him up.

As he pulled into Gran's drive, the place appeared deserted. Even the corner pub had looked empty as he drove past it. He turned the car off and removed his key from the ignition. The deep growl of the engine ceased as the headlights dimmed. David was plunged into darkness — there wasn't a single light on in the cottage.

David cautiously approached the front door, which had been left ajar.

'Grandma Rose? Are you alright?' David gently pushed the door open. Inside, he was shocked to find every table and chair had been turned upside down, every drawer emptied and scattered across the floor, and shattered glass covered the floorboards.

'Grandma Rose?' he called out, but there was no answer. David swallowed as a lump formed in the pit of his stomach. This was no burglary; he was sure of it.

At last, he found her tied up on the sofa, her complaints muffled by the gags stuffed in her mouth. He rushed over to untie her and wiped away her tears.

'Oh, David! He has the children and the Elves! Even my little Tammy!' she sobbed.

'Who has them?' David pressed urgently.

'King Summer! He was here waiting for them to come home. He had Dark Elves with him. Dark Elves! The man's gone insane — he couldn't possibly control them for long.'

David did not know what a Dark Elf was but assumed, whatever they were, they were bad news.

★★★

Laran pulled his phone out of his pocket as he jogged back to FERA. 'Hurleston, I need a clean-up team at my flat now.'

'Dark Elves?' Hurleston's voice resonated from the receiver, unfazed by Laran's abruptness.

'Yeah—three of them. They took Gail,' Laran answered, jogging along the corridor that led to Lilly's office.

'Goodness, this is chaos!' Lilly muttered to herself as she hurried to and fro in her office. Her computer continued to sound as more and more emails came in and her phone rang incessantly. Lilly inhaled slowly. To her surprise, King Autumn burst through the door.

'Lilly, what's going on?' Laran demanded.

'Laran! Sorry, I'm rather busy right now. King Winter's acting up again and I've got localised snow blizzards in Scotland. It's causing chaos! The Met office are furious! Can you come back later?'

Another phone on Lilly's desk started ringing, but before she could answer it, Laran placed a hand on the receiver.

'Lilly – it's important. And it's about the snow.'

Lilly noticed his heaving chest. 'Is everything alright?' she asked. 'What about the snow?' The phone suddenly stopped ringing, lulling the office into an unusual silence.

'Is David with the children?' Laran lowered his voice as he spoke.

'No,' Lilly began slowly, 'They're staying with my grandmother for the week. David's gone to pick them up now.' She paused, sitting down in her chair. 'Why?'

'I think they might be in danger, Lilly.'

'What sort of danger? What is this all about? I don't have time for riddles, Laran!'

'I think Taranis has kidnapped them again and is holding them in his castle – at the very heart of that blizzard.'

'What? How could you possibly know that?' Lilly narrowed her eyes at him.

'Because three Dark Elves have just taken Gail from my flat,' Laran said, raising his voice. 'We need to get to Scotland right now.'

'Hold on a second. Let me wrap my head around this – what do you mean?' Lilly began, as one of her assistants passed her the phone.

'Ma'am, it's your husband – he needs to speak to you urgently.'

Lilly took the phone with shaking hands. 'David?' Her demeanour changed as she listened to the frantic voice of her husband on the other end of the phone. Her body was limp by the time she put the phone down.

'King Summer and the Dark Elves broke into my grandmother's house and tied her up. They've taken the children and their Guardian Elves. They didn't stand a chance.'

'Why is Hyperion doing this? I haven't heard from him in about fifty years. What is he hoping to gain by kidnapping our children?' Laran put his hand on her shoulder, but Lilly pushed it away angrily, got up from her chair and paced her office, trying to collect her thoughts. After a few moments, she turned toward him.

'I have no idea why King Summer would want my children – or yours – but I am damned well going to find out. If he thinks he can stir up those blasted Dark Elves, we must set him straight. It is time the Elder Council realised I am Mother Nature,' Lilly declared. 'Gran is on her way to talk to Hurleston to persuade him to help us – but I think she's wasting her time. In the meantime, we're going to Scotland to get our children back…' Lilly stopped pacing and stood in front of Laran. She took another deep breath. 'Then we are going to bring the Elder Council back into line.'

'Yes, sir!' Laran agreed, shocked but impressed by this new decisive side to Mother Nature.

'Good,' Lilly said. 'I doubt Taranis and Hyperion will give the children up easily. This is probably going to lead to a full-on confrontation, if not worse. I suggest you gather your people together whilst I make some calls.' Lilly shut down her computer and marched past Laran, and out of her office.

Laran watched her go, finally allowing himself a small smile. *Fragile! Delicate! Solstice had to be joking*, he thought to himself.

CHAPTER SIX

Taranis was skulking about the castle, feeling even more wretched. His fight with Solstice was echoing in his head, and he was still feeling angry. He wasn't so much angry with her as with himself.

He couldn't believe that he had said those things to her or that, for a moment, he had considered hitting her. He desperately wanted to make it up to her, but what could he say? Truth be told, he wasn't sure he could bring himself to face her again just yet. He had been deliberately avoiding his study in case she was still in there. *That was his biggest problem*, he thought to himself bitterly. He was a coward. That was why he couldn't just apologise to Queen Winter for the things he had said, and that was probably why nobody respected him.

He was now in the back wing of the castle. He rarely came back here as it was mainly bedrooms. A quick glance out of the window showed it was still snowing. He wasn't doing that, though. It must be Solstice, he thought to himself. She was still here and, judging by the snow, she was very sad. He felt another pang of guilt and was about to turn around to look for her when he heard muffled shouting. Where was that coming from? He wandered along the corridor, past dark empty staterooms and various priceless oil paintings that dotted the walls. The sounds led him to the steps leading down to the dungeon.

★★★★

Someone was coming now, but Gail wasn't sure if he should be glad or not. What if it was one of the Dark Elves? Gail helped William up, who now held Willow in his arms. Being smaller, she was feeling the effect of the cold much worse. They shuffled back away from the door.

Gail stood in front of William, trying to protect him from whoever was coming. The door opened and Taranis walked in, looking very cross.

'What's all the noise?' he demanded, glaring at them furiously.

'We're freezing to death, my King,' Gail snarled, not at all intimidated by him.

'Please...' William begged, his hands shaking as much as his chattering teeth.

Gail glared at Taranis and then spoke to him in Elvish as he took Willow from William's arms and held her tight to his chest, trying to keep her slight frame warm. 'This is the Child of Nature. Even you can't be so stupid as to let her die.'

Taranis narrowed his eyes at him as William watched on in confusion. Although he couldn't understand what they were saying, he recognised the language.

'I know who she is, boy. I see you have the manners of your father,' Taranis retorted.

'When my father gets here, my manners will be the least of your problems,' Gail hissed back.

Taranis turned his gaze to the girl, who looked to be asleep. As much as his cowardly heart couldn't admit it, the boy was right. If anything happened to her, there would be hell to pay. But it was a mistake kidnapping Laran's boy — Taranis hated the Autumn Elves. Taranis's countenance suddenly changed as he anxiously chewed his nails. Hyperion would be furious if they died, let alone Mother Nature.

Not that he cared that much. However, Taranis shuddered at the thought of what Laran would do if anything happened to Gail. As far as Taranis was concerned, an angry Laran was far more dangerous than Hyperion and his Dark Elves put together.

Taranis relented. 'Come on, quickly. I'll take you somewhere warmer.'

'Thanks,' William muttered.

'Oh, you can talk now?' Taranis asked, bemused.

William ignored him as they traipsed out of the dungeon. The rest of the castle didn't seem to be much warmer at all. They could hardly even see out of the windows, which were almost frozen over by now from the snow that continued to fall outside. Even if they escaped, their fate outside was hardly reassuring.

Taranis threw them into the same room they stayed in last time they were at the castle.

'There are some sweaters in the closet. Light the fire if you're still cold.' For a second, it almost seemed like he cared about their wellbeing.

'King Taranis, how long are you going to keep us here? I want to go home. I'll tell my parents how kind you were so they won't be so cross with you,' William said in what he hoped was a very polite way.

Gail jumped in angrily, 'My dad will know where I am, and believe me, he will bring his army. You'll be very sorry you did this.'

Taranis couldn't stand that boy. He had a temper, just like his father.

'Sorry, but you must stay here.' Taranis left the room, locking the door behind him before their demands could sway him further.

The boys looked around the room; it was quite large with dark, wood-panelled walls. Two old armchairs sat in front of the grand marble fireplace and an enormous four-poster bed dominated the centre of the room. William put Willow into the bed while Gail put some jumpers on. He passed two to William. They were massive, but that didn't matter.

'Gail, you getting that fire going?' William asked as he kicked his shoes off and climbed into the bed, pulling Willow into his arms to warm her up.

'Should have it going in a moment. How's Willow?'

'Cold.' William rubbed Willow's arms vigorously.

Once the fire took hold, the room soon warmed up and their teeth stopped chattering.

'What now then?' William asked. It amazed him that he could hear. He suspected Gail was an Elf, but he was too polite to ask.

'We stay here, I suppose,' answered Willow, who finally had the strength to speak again.

'You mean,' William smiled in a foolish attempt to lift the mood, 'You don't have a plan?'

'No. We're probably going to be stuck in here for a while,' Willow moaned.

'Well, that's about right. Just when I was finally going to get a date with Suzy as well,' William sighed.

Willow smiled cheekily. William knew that smile. It was the one she used when she was about to suggest something he probably would not like.

Gail sat in one of the chairs, watching the brother and sister talking to each other. He pulled his phone from his pocket and frowned. No signal, damn it.

'So, Gail, your parents are members of the Elder Council?'

'Yeah, they are.' He hesitated, wondering where this was going, trying to drag his gaze away from her eyes. They were stunning. In fact, she was very pretty in an unusual way. Wisps of mahogany hair framed her delicate features. Her smile revealed a dimple on her chin. *Jeez Autumn, get a grip*, Gail thought to himself. *We're currently being held captive and you're drooling over a girl.*

'Gail, why are you sitting over there? Come and get warm,' Willow said. He was obviously attractive with his large brown eyes and auburn hair, offset by sun-kissed skin. Willow patted the space on the bed beside her expectantly. 'William and I are rather con-fused. Ever since you were brought to the dungeon, he can hear clearly. We're trying to figure out what's doing it,' Willow explained while Gail sat at the edge of the bed, untying his shoelaces.

'Normally, it's only the Guardian Elves that let me hear clearly. Are you a Guardian Elf? Although, you don't look like one.'

Gail hesitated a minute before he got up, kicked off his shoes and climbed into the bed. Willow moved up, allowing him to get in. She leaned against him, and he looked down at her shyly. Apart from Lilly's, he had never seen grey eyes like hers before. He put his arms around her. He wasn't used to this sort of easy intimacy. Willow was resting her head against his shoulder, as if she had known him all her life.

'I'm not a Guardian Elf, although it would be cool if I was. No, the reason that you can hear William is because I've opened the link between us,' Gail replied nervously, wondering how William would react to a virtual stranger in his head.

'You are an Elf, then?'

'I'm an Autumn Elf, which is why you don't recognise me. We're somewhat of an endangered species nowadays.'

'I thought only our Guardian Elves allowed William to hear. Not just any Elf?' It intrigued Willow.

'Well, no. Not any Elf… Didn't you know you are linked to me?'

'No, I didn't,' William answered slowly, trying not to let on how annoyed he felt, but knowing his voice sounded defensive. 'I didn't know you existed until today.'

'Well, my parents only told me last year.' Gail tried to make light of it all. 'You got drunk, I believe.' Gail raised a brow and William sniggered. Gail remembered it vividly. He was at Harvard, sat at the back of a rather dull lecture. But the longer he sat there, the stranger he felt. Eventually, something serious was going on; his head was swimming, and he couldn't move his legs. He got up to leave, but lost his balance entirely. He stumbled towards the door, only to throw up and collapse after two steps. The next day, he woke up back in Canada feeling very sick and nursing a pounding headache. 'I was sick in a lecture, quite embarrassing considering I'm underage in the US.'

'Oh, that must have been horrible.' Willow put her hand over her mouth in an unsuccessful attempt to contain her laugh.

'So how does it work? Will I be able to feel your moods?' William asked, irritated that

Willow wasn't appreciating the gravity of the situation.

'Yeah, but you can also close the link. My mum taught me how. She said to imagine a door in my head and to just shut it or open it if I need to know how you are. I knew when you were in the dungeon because I felt so cold. I tried to shut the link, but it didn't work. Takes practice.'

'So, it is the same as me and Heli.'

'Yes, but you and Heli don't have to try as you've been together since birth.'

'But why are you linked to William and who knows about this? Surely Mum doesn't? She'd never allow it.'

'I don't really know. I assumed it was because I'm King and Queen Autumn's son and William is Mother Nature's son. Strengthen alliances, that sort of thing,' Gail shrugged.

'But my parents don't know, do they?' William narrowed his eyes, confident that at least his dad would have told him.

Gail blushed. 'They must know. They would have had to agree to it.'

'Not necessarily. William is adopted; his birth parents could have done it.'

'Why would they have done that?' William snapped at Willow, who put her arms up in defence. 'My birth parents were ordinary Humans; they didn't know about any of this stuff.'

'I don't know then... I mean, my parents only told me because they had to, and they made it clear I should not share the information.'

'Well, let's just keep it between us as well then,' Willow announced to the boys, who nodded in agreement. 'Anyway, tell me about the twin incident, William!'

It was as Gail studied William's face that he realised William's eyes were the same colour eyes as his dad's. In fact, on closer inspection, William looked a lot like his dad.

'I wondered when you were going to bring that up. Is now really the time?' William groaned.

'Well, yes. It's not like we have any other pressing engagements, is it?' Willow tried not to laugh at the stricken look on William's face.

Gail smiled. He enjoyed listening to the pair of them. 'I was going to go for a drink with my cousin. I guess he has gone on his own now,' Gail mused.

'I love your accent. Where are you from?' Willow asked.

'Canada.'

'That's not a Canadian accent.' William scrunched up his nose in confusion.

'I went to university in the US for the last four years, so I guess I've picked up a slight American accent now,' Gail explained, sensing a little hostility from William.

'Which university did you go to?' Willow asked, elbowing William in the side for being rude.

'Harvard.' Gail wasn't sure why he wanted them to like him so much. He hadn't needed friends before.

'So, you've graduated already?' William narrowed his eyes at Gail. He didn't look old enough.

'Yes, earlier this year,' Gail observed William, who glared back at him. *Who were William's birth parents?* He thought to himself. *They had to be important. Why hadn't he met William until now? Why keep it a secret? And why did Mother Nature, of all people, adopt him?*

'How old are you?' William interrupted Gail's train of thought.

'William, that was rude.'

'No, it's fine. I'm nineteen. I went on a special scholarship.'

'Wow, you must be really clever,' Willow grinned as Gail blushed slightly. She turned her attention back to William 'So... Those twins!' Willow jibed as William sighed.

'Well, it was the day they all came over for tea. You had gone off somewhere with Jacen and Mum was chatting to Sarah in the kitchen...' William started and so began a very long-winded story of how the twins kissed and tormented William.

Soon after, the three of them grew sleepy, legs and arms intertwined together on the bed. It was odd how comfortable Gail felt with the two of them already. Getting kidnapped had an upside, clearly!

'William?' Willow asked.

'Yeah?' he grunted sleepily.

'Sorry about today.' Willow's voice had an air of sincerity to it.

'It's not your fault, Willow. It's all been a bit of a revelation today,' William chuckled softly. Relieved, Willow smiled and turned over to face Gail.

'Comfy?' Gail asked her with one eye open as he tentatively wrapped his arm around her.

'Yeah, you?'

'Uh huh,' Gail closed his eyes. He wondered who the Jacen was from William's story. *Probably her boyfriend*, he told himself, feeling jealous of someone he didn't even know.

★★★★

Laran stepped out of the tree and walked up Alectrona's drive, which was covered with perfectly manicured lawns and beautiful flowerbeds. Before he even got to the front steps, Alectrona opened the door. She was as striking as ever; her large, brown eyes flecked with gold, and her long, blonde hair was tied back and braided. Laran thought she was the most beautiful of all the Queens. But she was also the most distant and severe. She was almost exclusively seen wearing a smart business suit as she devoted herself to her work as the Queen of the Summer Fairies and her business empire. She spent almost every waking hour on the phone, in a meeting, or flying around the world for business. In fact, it surprised Laran he'd pinned her down at all.

'Laran, what a pleasant surprise. How are Andarta and Gail?' she said, inviting him into the sitting room.

'Andarta is well, but Gail. Well, I'm sorry to say your husband has kidnapped him,' he replied sternly.

Alectrona was taken aback. 'What? Goodness Laran, I'm so sorry. I thought he was still in self-imposed exile. I haven't heard from him at all.'

Laran nodded gravely. 'Yes, he's unfortunately favoured the support of the Dark Elves.

Alectrona looked embarrassed. 'Goodness, what is that man up to? Laran, can I get you anything? Tea, coffee perhaps? Or something stronger?'

'A coffee, please.'

'Of course.'

Laran followed her into the kitchen and watched as she bustled about, opening this drawer and that. Clearly, she didn't use it much.

'Now, tell me Laran. How can I be of help?' she asked, filling up the kettle. She smiled apologetically, gesturing flippantly around her, 'Sorry about this. The place is empty half the time.'

'It's fine; I was hoping you might know what Hyperion is up to. We assumed he'd spoken to you since he came back. Lilly's at her wit's end,' Laran said grimly.

'Lilly? You mean Mother Nature? I thought Solstice had warned you to stay away from her.'

Laran sighed in frustration and, sensing another confrontation, decided to beat Alectrona to the punch. 'I'm trying to avoid her, but that's been a little difficult lately with Hyperion and Taranis kidnapping our children. I haven't spent all these years keeping Gail safe for your husband to deliberately put him in harm's way,' Laran replied defensively, leaving Alectrona slightly off balance.

'Oh, well, in that case, maybe I was overzealous. I apologise, Laran,' Alectrona spoke rather sheepishly. 'But I still don't see how I can help you both.' She was slightly taken aback. Usually, he was so polite.

Laran felt a little guilty. He knew Alectrona liked him, although it annoyed him how she often treated him like a younger brother. She had, however, played the role of dutiful aunt to Gail, and he was immensely grateful for that. It had helped himself and Andarta bring Gail up as normally as possible. He watched as she spooned the coffee into two mugs and carefully added the boiling water.

'Milk, sugar?'

'Milk, one sugar, please.'

'Ah yes, now I remember,' she said as she got a bottle of milk from the fridge.

'I wanted to know if you had any idea what Hyperion was up to. He's your husband, after all; you must have some idea of what's driving him.' He thanked her as she passed him one of the mugs.

'I have as little knowledge of what my husband gets up to as you do. Ever since the fall of the Roman Empire, he's been awfully distant. I think all that being worshipped business really went to his head. I hadn't even realised he had come out of exile. Goodness me, this is embarrassing,' she sighed.

This made Laran smile. He had always had a bit of a thing for Alectrona; she was one of the few people that intimidated him a bit. Normally, it was the other way around. 'That's why I hoped you could help us out a little. You know, just come over and bring him back into line.'

'You know I would in a heartbeat, darling, but I just don't have the time now. I'm sure it's just another one of his silly phases. You know how he likes to get up to mischief. Give it a week. He'll get bored and move on to something else.'

'Well, I'm sorry to hear that,' Laran replied, finishing his coffee. 'But I don't think this is one of his phases. He's gone a step too far this time, kidnapping our children. But if you're busy, you're busy. There's nothing I can do about that. It was a pleasure as always, Ali,' Laran said before getting up to leave.

'I'm sorry I couldn't be of more help,' Alectrona said, as she showed him to the door.

Once Laran had left, Marcion – Alectrona's aide and second in command – walked into the kitchen with a grim look on his face.

'What's Hyperion up to now?' he asked.

'I have no idea, but I will not let him ruin years of my hard work,' Alectrona replied sternly. 'He isn't working alone, and Laran seemed to think he had been with the Dark Elves prior to this. Speak with the Emperor, make sure he isn't involved; this contravenes our agreement. If it's not the Emperor, try to find out who is pulling strings behind the Dark Elves's involvement. And keep tabs on those children!'

'Yes, I will have them all watched, especially Gail. Laran was foolish for bringing him to FERA,' Marcion replied grimly.

'Perhaps. But Gail needs to grow up, become a man. We can't treat him like a child forever.'

'What do we do if the Emperor is involved?'

'Then a petty skirmish between the Autumn and Winter Elves will be the least of our troubles. If the Emperor is behind this, then another Dark Elf War may be coming and we'll need every fighting Elf we can get our hands on.'

★★★★

One by one, Laran phoned the Autumn Lords and assembled an immediate council meeting at their administrative headquarters in Dusseldorf. By the time he arrived there, the three Autumn Lords were already waiting for him. Lord Veles and Astor saluted him as he entered, while Lord Umber merely dipped his head in respect.

'Gentlemen, I thank you for coming,' Laran began.

'What's the occasion, sir? Are the Dark Elves moving again?' Lord Astor asked.

'King Summer has kidnapped Gail with the help of King Winter. I need you to muster your forces and help me with a siege against King Winter's castle.'

'My King, the last war against the Dark Elves severely depleted our numbers. There are very few of us left. The Winter Lords must have a force of almost twenty thousand men. Between us, we will struggle to get close to ten thousand.' Lord Veles' brow was furrowed with concern.

'Do not forget our troops are hardened veterans. King Winter's armies have never seen combat. I highly doubt he will deploy all his troops in and around the castle. There are just too many of them. We can focus our forces into a spearhead and cut through their lines.' Laran felt confident as he announced his strategy.

'Let me get this straight; you want us to send our troops against an enemy that vastly outnumbers us, with a tiny chance of success and a strong chance that we'll all be slaughtered to the very last man?' Lord Umber asked.

'Yes,' Laran replied, his expression deadly serious, although the faintest smile played at the corner of his lips.

'Well, in that case, you can count me in. My troops are yours, my King,' Lord Umber declared.

'My forces are also at your disposal, my King,' Lord Veles said next.

The room fell silent as the three men turned to face Lord Astor, the youngest of the Lords. Lord Astor looked up at Laran, a fierce expression on his face.

'No.'

'Excuse me?' Laran replied.

'I will not grant you my troops for you to whittle away on some fool's errand. You drag us into one endless war after another. What will happen when there are no Autumn Elves left to fight your battles? Once you've warred us into extinction. We are not battle hardened; we are battle weary. The Winter Elves may not have seen a battle in some time, but they are formidable warriors.'

'Now see here!' Lord Umber roared, surging to his feet.

'No. You see here. The Autumn Elves are the most diminished of the four Elven houses. We've nothing more to give. My men will not be of service,' Lord Astor asserted, his face contorted with anger and disgust.

'Treason!' Lord Veles shot back. 'How dare you address your King in such a manner!'

'Let him be, Lord Veles. Are you certain, Lord Astor?' Laran asked, his voice deadly calm.

'I am certain.'

'I understand you do not want to get caught up in more conflict, Lord Astor. All three of you have paid dearly for your allegiance, and for that, I am immensely grateful. Is there another way you can help us, Lord Astor?' Laran asked.

'We have recently developed quite close ties with the Winter Elves. I can use my contacts to gather intelligence on their movements and numbers, and I will endeavour to provide as much logistical support as possible,' Lord Astor replied.

'That is all I ask for. Thank you, gentlemen. You may go.'

CHAPTER SEVEN

Lilly sat on the living room floor surrounded by maps of Scotland. She had to come up with some sort of plan to storm King Winter's castle. She took a bite out of some toast, lost in thought.

'Althea, I think we need Queen Summer. If anyone can get Hyperion into line, she can. I think we should split up.' Lilly looked at Althea, who murmured in agreement through a mouthful of toast, sending crumbs everywhere.

'Go and see Alectrona and let her know what Hyperion is doing. Hopefully, you'll be able to persuade her to come to the castle and give me a hand. Be polite and, of course, tell her about the children. Lay that on thick. Andarta might help too now that Gail is involved. Perhaps if we all show up together, Hyperion will back down.'

****

'So, what do you think about him?' William asked, as he sat up and yawned. Both Willow and William looked at Gail, who appeared to still be asleep.

'He's nice. Shy maybe.'

'Do you think we should tell Mum? You know, about this link?'

'Honestly, I don't know. Maybe Grandma Rose would be more pragmatic than Mum. She won't go off on one.'

'Is that why you were going to Gran's that morning?'

'It's easier to talk to Gran. She just listens, you know?'

William nodded in understanding. 'So, why do we trust him?' he made a flippant gesture towards Gail. 'He is an Elf.'

'What difference does that make? Give him a break, William.'

'Give *him* a break! Are you serious?' William signed furiously so Gail couldn't hear them. 'I've just found out a complete stranger has access to my head, and I'm the one that should give him a break?'

'Well, he's the one who deserves a break if he's spent that much time in your brain.' William glared at Willow, who sighed and took his hands in hers. 'William, calm down. This must be hard for him as well. I'll always have your back, but I don't think you need to worry too much about this.'

William breathed out, letting the tension leave his body. Willow snuggled back down next to Gail. She wondered what it would be like to kiss him. She had thought about kissing a lot since Jacen had kissed her. If she were honest, she had been a bit disappointed when Jacen had kissed her. It had been nice, but it wasn't mind-blowing. Maybe the problem was that she had no one else to compare it to.

'You really like him,' William teased her. 'He's way out of your league.'

'Oh thanks, William. I'm glad you think so highly of me.'

'What about Jacen? He told me he kissed you.'

'It was only one kiss,' Willow defended herself, although she wasn't sure exactly what she was defending. It wasn't like Jacen was her boyfriend. 'I don't know about Jacen. I thought I really liked him, but when he kissed me, I thought it would be, I don't know, more.' Willow shrugged and looked at William. 'I just can't imagine Jacen not being my friend. Maybe I just don't want to lose him as a friend. But I do find Gail attractive. Look at him. Who wouldn't?'

'He's bound to have a girlfriend. He's King Autumn's son. He probably spends all his time with rich socialites.'

'Well gee, William, thanks,' Willow muttered to herself, slightly annoyed.

William put some more logs on the fire before climbing back into bed. He noticed Willow had gone back to sleep. Either that or she was faking because she didn't want to talk to him anymore.

Gail, however, had woken up halfway through their discussion and realised they were talking about him, so quickly shut his eyes again and listened.

★★★★

Heli and Tammy had spent most of the night navigating the maze of hallways in the castle, avoiding any more Dark Elves and trying to work out where the children might be.

'Can you feel Willow?' Tammy asked Heli.

'Sort of, but the Dark Elves make holes in my connection to her. It's weird where the Dark Elves are. It's like the surrounding area is empty,' Heli tried to explain.

'Okay, so which way can you feel Willow the best?' asked Tammy.

'This way, I think.' Heli replied and started off down the right-hand corridor.

The two Elves wandered around the corridors for a long time. The castle appeared to be empty, except for the odd Dark Elf whom they avoided. Heli looked into some rooms before coming to a stop in front of one of them.

Tammy, who hadn't been paying attention, walked right into her. 'Why have you stopped?' she whispered indignantly.

'It's the kitchen,' said Heli.

'So,' replied Tammy.

'I'm hungry,' Heli explained, and pushed open the door.

'Is this really a good idea?' Tammy murmured, looking around.

'Of course, it is. If I'm hungry, William's bound to be,' Heli reasoned, walking over to the fridge, and started filling some bags she had found with easy-to-eat items.

Meanwhile, Tammy had found the larder and was ransacking it. 'Right, let's go,' she said. The two Elves quickly made their way out of the kitchen and back down the corridor. When they turned the next corner, to Heli's great relief, she finally knew where they were. They walked about halfway down the corridor until they were standing outside the door that Heli hoped was where Willow and William would be.

Heli quietly knocked on the door. She tried the door handle, but the door was firmly locked. Then she noticed the key was still in the lock. In his haste, King Winter had left it in the door. As she unlocked the door, Heli hoped she had the right room and that it wasn't instead filled with sleeping Dark Elves.

'Hurry,' whispered Tammy.

Heli glared at her, and then slowly pushed the door open. Tammy gently shut the door. She had taken the key from the other side and now locked the room from the inside.

The room was lit by the flames from the fire, but it was enough light for Heli to see that there was someone asleep in the enormous bed in the centre of the room. She tiptoed across and, to her utter relief, saw William's distinctive auburn hair poking out from under the covers. The two Elves emptied their bags onto a small side table. Then they took their shoes off and climbed into the bed, curling up under the covers and falling asleep.

★★★★

King Autumn crawled forwards on his belly through gorse and heather bushes to the crest of the hill. It was perfectly situated to give him an excellent view of King Winter's castle. He pulled out his binoculars and observed the scene below. Luckily for Laran, the snow had stopped at around two in the morning, probably at the same time King Winter had gone to sleep. It was six o'clock now and although it was overcast and cloudy still, he could see the castle and its grounds clearly.

A deep layer of snow covered the grounds, and they had dug a vast network of trenches out of it on the front lawn. Laran could see the Winter

Fairies, who resembled abominable snowmen patrolling the trenches, armed with weapons of various shapes and sizes. The weapons were all made from solid ice. They weren't alone either. All along the trench line were the Winter Elves, each of them dressed in full combat gear. They appeared relaxed, casually checking over their equipment, or just talking amongst themselves. Laran was about to lower his binoculars when he noticed something move slightly outside the trench system. It had only moved a bit, but it was enough for him to see that the Winter Elves were not the castle's only defenders. Large ice creatures were waiting, perfectly hidden in the snow, ready to ambush Laran's troops as they advanced. *Brilliant*, Laran thought to himself, not realising Taranis could lead such an underhand attack. Laran then turned and crawled down the hill until he was out of sight of the castle and back in his army camp.

All the Autumn Lords, save Lord Astor, were in the command tent when Laran walked in, including Aaron, Lord Umber's son and a few of the higher-ranking members of the army.

Aaron was Gail's cousin, and they looked very similar. They had the same dark auburn hair and classically handsome features. Although Aaron had a slightly smaller, crooked nose and bright blue eyes, instead of Gail's brown ones.

'How does it look, sir? When do we attack?' Aaron asked.

'Not yet. They are heavily dug in. The coming battle will be tough enough as it is, but with King Winter and King Summer here personally, it's going to be a massacre. We'll wait for Mother Nature to get here. Hopefully, she'll bring reinforcements.'

'Very good, sir. I have deployed our troops all around the castle and in the surrounding hills. But by our estimates, we are still a good five hundred Elves short of King Winter's army,' Lord Umber explained as he pointed out the positions of the Autumn forces on a map.

'Very good. I assume you've already tested their perimeter?'

'Yes, my King, the 58th infantry and I spent the better part of yesterday and this morning probing along the Winter Elves's line,' Lord

Veles interjected. 'Unfortunately, we struggled to find any noticeable weaknesses.'

'Hmm… If the children are being held in the castle, we can't use any form of artillery against it. The forward approach to the castle is slightly less defended, though. We don't have to capture or rout Taranis's army. I propose we launch a full offensive on the front of the castle and concentrate our forces in one place,' Laran said as he surveyed the map himself.

'Sir, if I may, it won't take long for Taranis's other forces to redeploy and engage us at the front. If they strike us in the flanks, there is a strong chance our forces will be defeated,' Lord Umber cautioned.

'I'm banking on Taranis's other troops redeploying. We'll strike the Winter Elves in a brutal and frontal all-out assault, which will hopefully frighten Taranis and his generals enough to redeploy the rest to repel us. Once they've done that, Aaron and his special-forces team will infiltrate the castle from the back right-hand side, locate the children and get them out.'

'I'll get my team together, sir.' Aaron saluted as he left the tent.

'Very good. Lord Umber, prepare the Sprites and Trolls. They'll be spearheading the assault. Lord Veles, you and the 58th will be the second wave. Are we all in agreement?'

'Yes sir,' the two Lords and their retainers echoed.

'Good. As soon as Mother Nature arrives, we attack.'

CHAPTER EIGHT

Hyperion opened his eyes and rose from his four-poster bed. He stretched and glanced out of the window and noticed, to his disgust, that it was snowing again. He walked into his en-suite, took a shower, and brushed his teeth before dressing himself in an impeccable cream suit.

'I think I'll check on my prisoners,' he said to himself as he strolled towards the dungeon. He didn't pass anyone on his way, which suited him fine. King Winter's temper tantrums were beginning to get on his nerves.

'And how are my prisoners feeling this morning?' he exclaimed in a long drawl. No response. He opened the cell door to find it empty. 'WHERE ARE MY PRISONERS?' he yelled to the empty room.

'WINTER!' he roared as he ran up the stairs to Taranis's office.

Taranis looked up and scowled as Hyperion marched in.

'Don't give me that look, you imbecile! Where are the children? I gave you one job!

One simple job and still you manage to screw it up! You have a gift, you know that? A gift for ineptitude!' Hyperion bellowed.

'Stop shouting at me, you unhinged lunatic!' Taranis shouted back. He was in no mood to be pushed around.

'Where are they? Somehow, three teenagers have outwitted you again. You, a one-million-year-old 'godlike' being, can't even keep track of three half-witted teenagers!' Hyperion roared, his spit flying everywhere.

'No, you moronic fool. I know exactly where they are. They were freezing to death when I checked on them last night. I locked them in the guest room, where it was a little warmer,' Taranis explained, doing little to hide his distaste that Hyperion was causing such a fuss over nothing. 'Laran is undoubtedly livid because you took his boy. I certainly didn't want to tell him we had accidentally killed him, too.'

'And why did you not deem it necessary to tell me? You know what, never mind. Take me to them now!' Hyperion ordered, still shaking with rage.

On their way to the guest room, one of the Dark Elves appeared.

'My Lord Hyperion, I must speak with you,' he said, a worried look on his face.

'What is it?' Hyperion asked impatiently.

'The Elves, my Lord, they have gone missing,' the Dark Elf replied.

'What?' Hyperion yelled.

'They attacked the guards after we had retired to our quarters,' the Dark Elf mumbled morosely.

'You useless waste of space! Get out of my sight! I shall deal with you all later.' Hyperion seethed and the Dark Elf rushed back the way he had come.

Taranis tutted, struggling not to laugh in Hyperion's arrogant face.

'Shut it and get this door open,' Hyperion scowled at him.

★★★★

William put another log on the fire. The temperature felt like it had fallen in the last half an hour, although it had stopped snowing outside.

As he made his way back to the bed, he noticed one of the side tables was laden with food.

'Willow did someone come in here last night?' he asked.

'I don't think so,' she answered sleepily, looking puzzled.

'Well, there're tons of food on this table and it definitely wasn't there last night.' William remembered just how hungry he was. Willow got off the bed to have a look and suddenly noticed the two sleeping Elves.

'William, it's Heli!' cried Willow with delight. 'How did they get in here?'

All the noise woke the two Elves and Gail up.

'How did you get here?' asked Willow, hugging Heli.

'With the power of nature!' giggled Heli.

'Are we still locked in?' said William through a mouthful of bread.

Tammy proudly held up the keys.

'Oh, you clever girl!' said Gail.

Tammy looked at Gail, not registering him before, with a look of shock on her face.

'Gaillardia, what are you doing here? Has anyone recognised you?' Tammy asked in rapid-fire Elvish, so Willow and William wouldn't understand.

'The Dark Elves snatched me, and no, they don't know who I am. They just think I'm Laran's pet Elf,' Gail replied in Elvish.

'You need to get out of here before you're recognised!' Tammy said urgently. To reassure him, she reached over and squeezed his hand. 'You look so much like your mum.'

William looked at Willow. 'Do you know what they're saying?'

'No, it was too fast. Heli shut our link.' Willow frowned.

Gail turned his attention to Willow and William. 'I should escape and find my dad. I'm the only one not wearing shorts, after all!' Gail laughed a little, looking at the others. 'These woolly sweaters aren't enough to protect you from the snow. You'll get frostbite.'

'I agree. Gail is our best chance of getting out of here.'

'Well, if that's our only option,' Willow replied before turning to Gail. 'When we were here last time, there was a door leading to the rose garden. It should be unlocked. Be careful,' she said shyly, giving him a quick hug and locking the door behind him.

Gail ran down the corridor, but as he rounded the corner, he came across a pair of Winter Elves.

'Crap how am I going to get past those two?' he muttered under his breath as the Winter Elves unknowingly marched towards him. He retraced his steps before ducking into a side room and closing the door behind him. He stood leaning against the wall next to the door frame, waiting for them to pass. It was only after they passed, he noticed the contents of the room he was in. Judging by the table and chairs stacked against the far wall, it was once some sort of stateroom. Now, however, it was packed with various boxes and cases. Upon closer inspection, the boxes were full of all sorts of military supplies, ranging from bandages and medical equipment to weapons and ammunition. Gail had an idea.

After fifteen minutes of going through them, he'd gathered all the clothes and equipment necessary for him to pass off as a Winter Elf. He started with a pair of dark brown hiking boots, followed by some camouflaged trousers and a hooded waterproof jacket. Then he wore a white balaclava with a single slit for the eyes, trying to cover as much of his tanned, dark skin as possible. He finished his disguise with a pair of tinted sunglasses and ballistic gloves. There was no mirror in the room, so Gail prayed no one would pay too close attention to him. He quickly grabbed a combat helmet and some tactical webbing and cautiously crept out of the room, walking brusquely back up the corridor towards the door Willow had told him about.

Luckily, it was unlocked, and he pulled it open, expecting it to lead out onto the lawn. Instead, it opened to reveal a trench network dug out of the metres-thick snow. He kept his head down as he attempted to walk casually through the Winter Elf ranks. They were busy preparing their weapons and readying themselves for the coming battle. As he was wondering how to get out of the trench to the cover of the woods, someone grabbed him by the shoulder.

'Private, what are you doing?' A gruff-looking Winter Elf sergeant asked.

'Erm... Just marching back from the latrine sir,' Gail quickly bluffed.

'Where are you posted?'

'Erm, with the err, by the...' Gail stammered.

'It doesn't matter. You've just been reassigned. The Autumn Elves have been probing our lines for the past day, and it's time we took the fight to them. I'm leading a team on a raid into the forest to see if we can catch any of the Autumn Elf scouts with their pants down. The rest of the men are getting ready in that dugout over there. Go join them, private,' the sergeant ordered.

'Yes sir,' Gail replied and hurried off towards the dugout that the sergeant had indicated. He walked in to find four Winter Elves checking their weapons. One of them, a corporal, looked up as he entered and walked over.

'You must be our new number six. I'm James. Nice to meet ya.'

'Oh, hi I'm G-Graham, it's nice to meet you... sir,' Gail stuttered as he tried to think up a false name. Corporal James gave him a funny look. 'Where's your firearm, private?'

Gail swallowed as he looked at him, flustered. He was internally kicking himself for forgetting to take one from the supply room.

'Never mind. There's a spare M16 on the table over there. Grab it before the sergeant gets in here.'

No sooner had Gail picked up the carbine than the sergeant walked in and ordered them to move out.

They left the trenches and quickly ran across the no-man's-land between the castle and the forest. Once there, they spread out and carefully crept between the trees, alert for any sign of the Autumn Elves.

They continued like this for ten minutes when suddenly all hell broke loose. The crack of gunfire from somewhere up ahead caused the entire squad to drop to the ground.

'Return fire!' the sergeant yelled as Gail crawled on his belly into a ditch. Bullets whizzed overhead and a grenade went off nearby, sending dirt and pine needles through the air. James was nowhere to be seen, and the rest of the squad were shooting towards where they thought the Autumn Elves might be.

Realising he wouldn't get a better chance, Gail crawled along the ditch, away from the Winter Elves, before dashing through the trees and away from the fighting.

Ten minutes later, he was thoroughly lost. He leaned against a tree to get his breath back. As he was leaning there, he heard the crack of a twig. He peered round the tree, gun raised, but couldn't see anyone. Gail sighed, going back to his original position only to be confronted by the muzzle of an assault rifle and a furious-looking Autumn Elf. He was kitted out in brown and green camouflage, a balaclava covering his face like Gail.

'Drop the weapon,' Aaron ordered.

'Aaron? Get that thing out of my face. It's me, you muppet!' Gail laughed, dropping his gun on the ground.

'We've met?'

'It's me, Aaron,' Gail replied, removing his helmet and balaclava.

'Gail? What are you doing dressed up as the enemy, you twit? I almost shot you!'

'It's a disguise, you idiot! I had to sneak past all those Winter Elves.'

'Yeah, I bet. You spend two minutes in Taranis's castle, and you've already defected. Come on. Your dad's tent is this way. He will be furious when he hears you've sided with the enemy,' Aaron joked, leading Gail back through the woods.

King Autumn looked up from the maze of maps surrounding him as Gail entered the tent. He had changed out of the Winter Elf uniform and was now wearing Autumn army camouflage and armour instead.

'Gail? Where on earth did you come from?' exclaimed Laran, wrapping Gail in a spine crushing hug.

'I missed you too, Dad.' Gail grinned, hugging him back.

'Are you alright? Did they hurt you?' Laran placed his hands on Gail's shoulders so he could examine him further. 'I've been so worried. You're going straight back to Canada when this is all over.' Laran pulled Gail into another hug.

'I'm fine, Dad. They didn't hurt me.' Gail blushed as he realised all eyes were on them. 'And that won't be necessary. I think Hyperion just took me to annoy you,' Gail tried to reassure his father.

'So, how did you get out? Where are Willow and William?' Laran asked, looking behind Gail and expecting to see the siblings standing there.

'I'm not sure I have time to tell you the full story. Aaron briefed me on the plan. I want to take his place,' Gail answered as he walked over to look at the map of the castle.

'No way. You've just got out of there. I'm not sending you straight back in,' Laran declared.

'Dad, think about it. Your head-on offensive will not rout the Winter Elves. At best, it's just going to buy us some time to sneak into the castle. I've already been inside. I know where Willow and William are being held. If I'm leading the team, we can sneak in, grab them, and sneak out again before anyone's the wiser,' Gail argued pragmatically.

Laran was silent for a moment before coming to a decision.

'Fine, just be careful. Alright?'

'Yes sir,' replied Gail as one of his men passed him a note.

'Mother Nature and Queen Winter have arrived,' Gail informed Laran.

'Excellent, show them in,' Laran replied, without looking up. He was studying a more detailed map of the castle now, looking for any hidden passages he could use to sneak Gail and his men in.

Gail left the tent and strode towards the entrance of the camp. It had taken King Autumn and his forces about a day to set up camp, which was complete with an armoury and medical facility. It was currently seething with armoured Elves and Tree Sprites. All of them were busily prepping for battle.

Mother Nature and Queen Winter stood at the entrance to the camp. Queen Winter's expression was unreadable. She had been involved in campaigns with Laran before and wasn't particularly happy that this one was against her home. Lilly was very surprised at the entire operation. It seemed as if a small, tented village had sprung up almost overnight. In her experience, you couldn't sneeze these days without media attention. *Lord Hurleston must work very hard to keep this under wraps,* she thought.

'Gail, I thought they snatched you as well!' Lilly exclaimed.

'I escaped earlier with the help of your Guardian Elves.'

'Willow and William, are they alright?'

'Yes, they're fine. We will get them back safe. Don't worry, Lilly.'

Lilly smiled at him as he led them into the tent.

'Mother Nature, Solstice, it's good to see you. I trust you have brought reinforcements,' Laran greeted them. Lilly noticed Laran was wearing body armour with a sword strapped at his side. His other Elven lieutenants flanked him.

'I have a group of my most loyal Winter Elves ready to assist your forces in the battle,' Queen Winter replied. 'Unfortunately, all the Winter Lords have already pledged their allegiance to my dimwit husband, so I could only rally about a hundred of them.'

'That's unfortunate, but it'll have to do. I will, however, need you to help me out with this snowstorm. If you can, I'd like you to make it as vicious as possible until my Elves have closed with the enemy. That should completely reduce the Winter Elves's line of sight, making their trenches irrelevant.'

'I can do that,' Solstice replied with a nod.

'Excellent. The 58th infantry will lead the attack after the Sprites and Trolls. Once they've closed with the enemy, Lilly, I'd like you to work with Solstice in overpowering Taranis and dropping the snowstorm completely.'

'Yes, I can do that.'

'And Lilly, I have yet to hear the entire story, but Gail assured me he knows exactly where Willow and William are. They're fine and in bizarrely good spirits. The Guardian Elves are with them. Gail's volunteered to go in and get them.' Laran smiled in the hope he had reassured her.

It occurred to Lilly that Laran probably spent most of his time as a general, but despite what she had said earlier, she didn't want to fight unless she had to. She suspected Laran enjoyed this sort of thing and would be more than happy to forgo a diplomatic solution. She had to make sure he knew she was in charge here. Otherwise, this could end badly.

'When are you planning on attacking?' Lilly asked.

'Well, now that you're here, as soon as the Elves are ready and I give the order,' Laran replied, his expression stern.

'Don't attack yet. I want to talk to Taranis and Hyperion first. Solstice and I still think that we can reach a diplomatic solution, and I'd much prefer to get my kids back through peaceful negotiation than violence.'

'Mother Nature, with all due respect, the time for negotiation has passed. My forces have already repeatedly engaged the enemy and to go out there now would be dangerous, let alone foolhardy,' Laran argued.

'Well, I disagree. We'll travel under a white flag and attempt to negotiate a peaceful resolution to all this foolishness. And as Mother Nature, my word is final,' Lilly ordered calmly, making it clear she wanted no further argument.

Laran sighed dramatically. 'So be it. But only under the condition that Queen Winter goes first and warns them of our intentions. Obviously, the Winter Elves are far less likely to shoot you on sight than us.'

'Gladly, Laran,' Solstice replied with a grim expression.

'All you need to do, Solstice, is tell them I'm coming and make sure Taranis's troop have stood down. Once they have, I'll try to negotiate my children's return with Taranis,' Lilly told her confidently.

'Wait, what about me? There is no way you are going in there alone,' Laran said.

'I won't be alone; I'll have Solstice with me. And I don't want Taranis or Hyperion feeling threatened whilst I'm trying to negotiate with them. Besides, don't you have army stuff to do here?'

'The army can take care of itself for a little while. I don't like the idea of you going in there with just Solstice for back up. Either you take me with you, or you don't go at all.'

Lilly sighed. 'Laran, I'm Mother Nature, possibly the most powerful person on this planet. You and I both know I could take back my children without your assistance.'

Laran swallowed. 'Yes, I know that, but would you ruin this entire plan just to prove your point?'

'Laran, with a flick of my wrist, I could render every living thing unconscious for a hundred miles. But I would rather find out why Taranis and Hyperion are doing this.'

'Lilly, just let me come with you.'

'Fine just let me do the talking,' Lilly compromised. *Silly man,* she thought, *I'm the one that protects him and every other living thing on this planet.*

CHAPTER NINE

Lord Hurleston was sitting at his desk, wading through all the angry emails about the snow in Scotland. Most of them were from members of the Met Office, who were most upset at King Winter for making them look like a bunch of fools... Again.

Damn King Winter, he thought. *What was wrong with the man? Did he not realise that the Humans noticed things like blizzards in the middle of what was in line to be the hottest August since records began?* Hurleston sighed. On the plus side, at least King Autumn and Mother Nature had finally teamed up to bring Summer and Winter back into line. Perhaps Lilly could reunite all the fairy kingdoms and sort all this mess out.

It was as Lord Hurleston sat ruminating that he noticed the ruckus going on outside his door. What could be going on at this late hour? As far as he was aware, he was the only person left in the building, except for security. The moment he stood up from his desk and walked to the door, it flew open and in marched Lilly's grandmother, followed closely by two very upset security Elves.

'Ah Rose,' said Lord Hurleston in his most placating voice as she marched across his office. Lord Hurleston dismissed the two security Elves, reassuring them he could deal with his unexpected visitor.

'Rose,' he began, 'to what do I owe the pleasure at such an ungodly hour?' He watched as she sat down in his chair, clearly deliberately. *She always was a tricky one*, he thought to himself. He sat down opposite her in the visitor's chair and rested his elbows on the desk.

'Don't give me all that, Jasper,' she said, as if talking to a two-year-old. 'Are you so out of touch these days that you haven't noticed the crisis unfolding in your own department? My goodness, things have got shoddy since I left,' she replied, in a very cross and patronising tone.

'You've completely lost me, Rose,' he said puzzled, wondering what on earth he could have missed that had resulted in him now having a furious ex-Mother Nature sitting in his office. As bull-headed and dogmatic as she was, he had missed her ever since Lilly had taken over as Mother Nature and couldn't stop the small smile which played at the corner of his lips.

'That dreadful King Summer broke into my house yesterday and snatched my grandchildren.' Now she was madder than a hornet's nest that had just been kicked. 'And as if that wasn't bad enough, he had Dark Elves with him. Dark Elves! Is the man deranged? No one can control those awful creatures!'

Lord Hurleston got up and walked over to his kettle in the corner. He kept it in his office for stressful occasions such as these.

'Why don't I make us some tea, and perhaps between the two of us, we can sort this out?' he suggested, while filling the kettle from a jug of water and turning it on. Looking around, he noticed Tammy was nowhere to be seen. 'Where is Tammy?'

'Oh, and they took the Elves! Why do that? What use are they to them?' said Rose as Lord Hurleston passed her a cup of tea.

'Well, that would probably explain Scotland, then.'

'What about Scotland?' asked Rose.

'Oh, King Winter is causing violent snow blizzards in Scotland. I suspect that's where King Summer has taken the children.'

'So, what are you going to do about it, Jasper? I seem to remember Lilly coming to see you just last week to tell you those two were up to something.'

'Rose, what can I do about it now? Lilly and King Autumn have already left for Scotland.'

'Jasper, you can't just sit idly by while Lilly needs your help,' protested Rose. 'And did you say King Autumn? You have sent my granddaughter to Scotland with Laran? Have you gone completely mad? Have you forgotten Holly already?' she exclaimed, struggling to retain her composure.

'Rose, I can't step in. Lilly must do this on her own, or else she will never have control of the Elder Council. Surely you must see that. As regrettable as it was, what happened to your daughter was out of my hands. She told my people she didn't need our assistance and, as she was acting Mother Nature at the time, I took her word for it. I have explained all of this to you before, and I fail to see what relevance it has to our current predicament,' Lord Hurleston explained curtly. Despite what he had just said, he still felt guilty for his part in what had gone on all those years ago and often refrained from talking about it.

'As for Laran, he's a changed man now and has put all that behind him. They took his son and he is possibly in more danger than Lilly's children. Lilly is not Holly, and she appears to handle Laran well. In some respects, I think it will be good for them.'

Rose nodded. 'Sorry Jasper, that was rude of me. I see your point. I just don't want history to repeat itself. When we lost Holly, it almost destroyed us all, especially Laran. And what was Andarta thinking bringing young Gaillardia here? We haven't spent all these years hiding that boy for one of Hyperion's tantrums to ruin our plan. Does he know who the boy is?'

'I don't think so. Anyway, this is a chance for Lilly to really flex her muscles as the new Mother Nature. She can finally assert her authority over the Elder Council by bringing Hyperion and Taranis back into line. It will all pan out, and it will be good for her. Just give it time.'

They sat in silence for a while until Rose finished her cup of tea.

'Thank you, Jasper. I had almost forgotten how much I enjoyed our little sparring matches.'

Lord Hurleston smiled. 'As had I,' he said, showing Rose to the door. 'Please, if there is anything else I can help you with, don't hesitate to ask.'

Rose stopped and turned to Lord Hurleston. 'Well, there is one small thing,' she said.

'Go on,' he invited, more than a little intrigued.

'When King Summer snatched the children, he showed a peculiar interest in William. I don't think he made the connection, but it's only a matter of time. William is the spitting image of his father.'

'I see. Don't worry. I will discreetly speak to those concerned. How is the boy? Is he showing any signs?'

'He is delightful. Although he looks like his father, he has his mother's gentle nature. I don't

think he'll give us the problems his father does.'
Rose paused in thought for a moment. 'No, I
have noticed nothing, but it's early still. He is
only eighteen.'

Lord Hurleston nodded in understanding
as he walked Rose to the lifts. 'Are you going
back to Dorset tonight, Rose?'

'No, I'm staying at Lilly's flat tonight and
travelling back tomorrow,' Rose said as she
stepped into the lift.

'Ah! Very wise.' And with that, the doors
closed, and she was gone.

★★★★

Queen Winter walked calmly through the
snow that was now covering the front lawns of
the castle. The Winter Fairies had growled at
her as she passed but had done nothing more.
Their growling had bothered Solstice, though,
and she made a mental note to give King Winter
a piece of her mind when she got inside. Why
was King Winter doing this? She sighed sadly
as she thought of her prized roses, now crushed
and buried deep in the snow.

Her anger only increased as she remembered how they were both meant to go to the southern hemisphere together to oversee the Winter there. They had planned to spend some time together, a romantic holiday. Solstice kicked some snow angrily. What upset her the most was that she had had to fly all the way back to Scotland from Australia to sort out her misbehaving husband. She walked through the imposing oak doors of the castle to find – much to her distaste – five Dark Elves waiting for her.

'Excuse me, miss. What business do you have here?' one of them asked.

'What business? This is my home, you insolent little fiend,' she spat before fixing him with an icy blue stare that froze him solid. 'Now fetch my husband and King Summer,' she demanded of the other Dark Elves, who wasted no time scurrying away.

★★★★

'If you don't open this door right this second, you ghastly children, I'll have King Winter super cool the lock and shatter it. And since you've wasted our time, we will not be gentle. You don't want that now, do you?' King Summer insisted calmly, despite his burning inner rage. King Winter was merely sulking beside him.

Hyperion was about to make him come good on the threat when four of the five Dark Elves appeared.

'What do you want now?' Hyperion exclaimed.

'My Lord, Queen Winter is here and wishes to speak to you both,' one replied.

'Oh god…' Taranis moaned, massaging his temples.

Hyperion sighed. 'Is she? Well, best not keep her waiting! I suspect King Winter is in enough trouble as it is. Guard this door. Make sure nothing comes out or goes in.'

'Queen Winter, you look as entrancing as ever,' Hyperion flattered her as he walked into the main hall.

'Shut up, Hyperion. You repulse me. I'm not here to speak to you. Frankly, I'm beginning to wonder what you're still doing in my house.' Queen Winter could scarcely hide the disgust on her face.

'Come now, there's no need to be so rude. King Winter and I are about to do great things,' he replied.

'I wouldn't count on it,' she replied dismissively before turning to Taranis. 'Taranis my love, please quit this foolishness; can't you hear what he's saying? The man's unhinged,' Queen Winter pleaded with King Winter.

Taranis stepped forward solemnly, his voice low. 'I cannot, Solstice. The die is cast, and I have made my choice. Why don't you join us? We could change this world together, darling.'

'Are you insane? This is childish madness. Just give it up! Release the children. Mother Nature is reasonable. I can convince her to forgive you. Please Taranis, you're breaking my heart,' Solstice's voice strained as she begged, tears rolling silently down her face.

King Summer laughed at the pitiful display in front of him. 'Even if he wanted to, I won't let him. I'm in control around here.'

'The children must stay here,' King Winter agreed.

'Well, in that case, order your forces to stand down and allow Mother Nature and King

Autumn to enter the castle so that formal negotiations may begin,' Solstice said. Her tone was
now unreadable, and her voice detached once
more.

'King Autumn is here? That will make things
a lot more interesting,' King Summer mused
with a smile. He was looking forward to putting his infamous military prowess to the test.
'You can inform them it is safe to approach.'

Queen Winter marched out of the room
without as much as a backwards glance at King
Winter, who stood cowering in the corner,
miserable and alone.

CHAPTER TEN

William stood on a chair and peered out of the window.

'Can you see anything?' asked Willow impatiently.

'No, hang on a minute,' he said as he wiped the windowpane with the sleeve of his over-sized sweater. 'Nope, nothing, just loads of snow and those weird snow animal things. Looks like we're stuck here. We wouldn't last five minutes out there in shorts, sorry Willow.'

'What about an Elf?' said Willow looking at Heli and Tammy, both of whom were trying to hide as they most definitely didn't want to go out there. William shook his head. 'Snow's too deep. We just have to trust Gail,' he said.

'Oh,' was all Willow said as she sat back on the bed. They had been here for two days. Where were Mum and King Autumn? Why hadn't they come and rescued them yet? What if Gail hadn't made it? No, she mustn't think like that. She pulled the surrounding covers, wishing Gail were still here.

'Heli, can you tell if there are Dark Elves outside?' William asked.

Heli closed her eyes and concentrated. It was harder to detect the Dark Elves because Willow appeared to be asleep. Finally, Heli nodded.

'I think they're outside the door,' she said.

Damn, thought William. They were running out of food, and it looked like a trip to the kitchen was out of the question. He pulled the blankets around him and decided to have a nap as well.

★★★★

Hyperion sat in Taranis's throne, smirking as Mother Nature, King Autumn and Queen Winter entered the hall. King Winter stood meekly to the left of Hyperion.

'Mother Nature, it's good to see you. And look at you! You're looking so well,' Hyperion announced loudly.

'Enough games, Hyperion. Where are my children?' Lilly demanded, ignoring his imprudent coquetries.

'Why is everyone being so rude to me lately? It really is quite upsetting. It doesn't set a good example for the children to follow now. And I must confess, their manners have been quite atrocious as of late.'

'I'll ask you once more, where are my children? There will be no negotiations unless I am satisfied that they are alive and well,' Lilly replied calmly. Her refusal to rise to his taunting had caused King Summer to stop smiling.

'Fine. Taranis take her to the children,' he instructed. 'But not you,' he said as King Autumn followed them. 'You can stay here.'

'I want to see if my son is alright,' Laran didn't want Hyperion to know that Gail was safe already.

'I'm sure Mother Nature can check on him for you.' Hyperion waved a hand dismissively.

King Winter led Lilly and Solstice to the guestroom.

'Unlock it then,' Lilly demanded.

'I can't. I don't have the key.'

'What do you mean you don't have the key?' Lilly replied incredulously, losing all patience with him. Lilly knocked on the door. 'Willow, it's Mum, are you alright?' she called through the door.

'Mum, is that really you?' Willow replied drowsily.

'Yes, darling. Open this door so I can see you both.' Lilly heard a clunk as Willow unlocked the door and popped her head out to make sure it was really her. On seeing her mum, Willow pulled the door wide open and flew into Lilly's arms. William was standing behind her, staring coldly at King Winter, his hands balled into fists.

'Where is the other boy?' Taranis asked, looking at the two children, and trying desperately to evade William's angry glare. He could see how badly William wanted to hit him. *And who could blame him?* thought Taranis.

'He escaped. He's told his dad everything.' William's face was the picture of disdain.

King Winter cleared his throat impatiently. 'Haven't we got some business to attend to?' he asked Lilly, causing Queen Winter to glare at him.

'Yes, kids. I need you all to stay here for a bit longer while I talk to King Summer. Then I'll be right back to get you. Okay?'

'Are you serious, Mum?' William exploded at her. 'You've come here to save us and now you're asking us to be prisoners for "a bit longer"?'

'I'm sorry, darlings. You'll be safe here, won't they, Taranis? Just don't leave, no matter what, okay?'

'They won't be able to leave as young Willow here is going to give me back my keys, aren't you?' King Winter asked, holding out his hand.

Willow stood there, scowling at him. 'Mum, tell him!' she complained.

'There's no point arguing, sweetheart. Just give him the key,' Lilly said and with that, Willow handed it over.

'Thank you,' Taranis said, taking the key. He closed the door on a shocked Willow and William and locked it. This time, he put the key in his pocket.

'King Summer awaits!'

Lilly sighed in response as she trudged after him, Solstice in tow.

★★★★

As soon as they had left to check on the children, King Autumn's calm façade evaporated. He rounded in on King Summer.

'Hyperion, what the hell do you think you're doing?' he demanded.

'I don't know what you're talking about, brother dear,' Hyperion replied, trying to sound innocent and confused.

'Don't give me that rubbish. What are you up to? Since when do you go around kidnapping children and working with Dark Elves? You used to hate them just as much as I do.'

King Summer let out an exasperated sigh. 'Don't you tire of it all? Don't you ever just get sick of all this, all this fighting, and all these petty political power plays that go on all the time? I'm bored, Laran. I'm sick and tired of it all and I want it to end!'

'What? What are you talking about? Perhaps if you did your job properly instead of spending all your time hiding away from the world doing nothing, you wouldn't be so bored. What happened to the man that used to fight at my side? What happened to the glorious King Summer, greatest of all the Elder

Council?' Laran demanded, his voice dripping with incredulity.

'I woke up. I woke up, and I realised it's all pointless! None of it's worth it in the face of eternity! You and the others all going around like you're privileged and special, like you're godly and gifted. Well, we're not, are we? We're cursed to live forever, never changing, always the same with no way out. I'm sick of it. I don't see why we should bother anymore. It was all right at first, when we thought we were the chosen few, the gifted, but this isn't a reward, is it? It's a punishment I don't think we deserve. I mean, look at the Humans and the Elves, so wrapped up with their own fleeting, petty lives. They don't need us anymore, and they don't want us, do they? Not really. I mean, look at you, still interacting, still getting involved. Why, what's the point? When everything we do for them eventually crumbles away to nothing.'

'Well, I suppose I do it so that I don't end up like you. Mad and alone, with no stake left in this world. This punishment you talk about, this suffering you've had to endure, it's all self-inflicted. It's all been at your own hand, no one else's. Perhaps if you engaged a little more, perhaps if you tried to connect with the world again, you might find a reason to go on. But if you stay like this, Summer, if you keep hiding away, passively watching the world go by, you'll soon be replaced.' Laran was trying desperately to make King Summer see sense and stop his stupidity.

It was at that moment that King Summer suddenly realised something. No... Could it be? Surely not? If it was, then things were about to get very interesting. If Hyperion's hunch was correct, then life might be worth living after all.

'It's alright for you Laran,' Hyperion went on, changing his tact. 'It's suddenly become clear to me you might have quite a vested interest in the Humans. Especially with this new Mother Nature and some very specific members of her immediate family. Let alone the Elf boy. Don't think I don't know who he is, what he is even. It's a very dangerous game you and Alectrona are playing,' Hyperion hissed at him.

'What are you talking about?'

'Come now, Laran. I'm no fool. You couldn't hide that sort of thing forever.'

'I'm not hiding anything,' Laran replied indignantly.

Before Hyperion replied, Lilly, Solstice, and Taranis returned.

King Summer jumped to his feet excitedly. The next couple of years were going to be a lot of fun indeed.

'Well, are you satisfied? Can we begin?' he asked eagerly.

'I want you to give me back my children. Why are you doing this? I don't understand, nor frankly, do I have time for this nonsense,' Lilly announced.

'And if I refuse?'

'Why would you refuse? Explain to me how kidnapping my children and holding them here in these appalling conditions is going to make me do whatever you want so badly. When you and I both know I can destroy all of this and you in a second.' She spoke calmly but firmly, looking him straight in the eye.

'You would do that? Knowing the children are inside? You would risk their safety?' King Summer still felt he had the upper hand here. 'Would you do that knowing that the children are inside, Laran?' He asked, turning to King Autumn, who just scowled. 'No, I thought not.'

Lilly sighed in frustration. 'Okay, Hyperion. What do you want?'

'Oh, come on. You know what I want. You alone have the combined powers of the entire Elder Council put together, as well as the ultimate authority over all four seasons. With a click of your fingers, you could batter the Humans with tornadoes, hurricanes, and wildfires. All more destructive than anything they have ever seen. You could render them all infertile over night or even ravage them with plagues. In short, you are a superweapon.'

'Excuse me?'

'The Humans are trashing this planet, assaulting our kingdoms with their ignorance and reckless stupidity. I just want you to carry out a minor culling, just a little one. A couple of million or maybe even a billion to put them back in their place and give us a fighting chance. Otherwise, a hundred years from now, that's it for the Elves.'

Lilly laughed coldly. Laran looked at her worriedly. Things were not going according to plan, and if Lilly couldn't convince Hyperion to back down, he wasn't sure he'd be able to force him to.

That hadn't been the reaction Hyperion had been expecting, either. Perhaps his sources had been wrong about this new Mother Nature. When he had gone into exile, Rose had only just become Mother Nature and Lilly wasn't even on the scene. As far as he was concerned, she was meant to be gentle and kind, the traits he considered weak. He thought he could boss her around and blackmail her. If it turned out he had misjudged her, then this whole venture could blow up in his face.

'No, Hyperion, I won't. Frankly, this conversation is a waste of my time.'

'What? Is that it then? You're just going to let the children die?'

'No, because I don't think you're actually going to kill them, Hyperion. You're all talk. You must have known this would never work. There's no chance I'm going to help you kill a part of the Human population, the same way there's no chance you're going to kill my children.'

'And what makes you so sure of that?' Hyperion asked, his voice dripping with contempt.

'Because you're still afraid of me, aren't you? Beneath your veneer of superiority, you're still afraid of all that power you gave to my ancestors all those years ago. You're still very much afraid of what it could do if someone made me angry enough to use it properly.'

'How dare you! I am an Immortal, I fear nothing, I...'

'ENOUGH! You have wasted too much of my time already and to be honest, it's insulting. To think that you have the audacity to come back from a fifty-year exile and start throwing your weight around, making demands, and trying to extort me? Clearly you will not see sense, so this discussion is over. Solstice, Laran, we're leaving.'

Hyperion sat there, dumbstruck. He took a long pause before letting out a sinister laugh.

'Is that it? You've said what you had to say, laid down the law and now you're just going to walk out of here?' Lilly ignored him. 'You think I'm going to let you leave?' He was becoming desperate now.

Lilly ignored him again. Hyperion's meagre façade of control cracked completely and was replaced by cruel hatred. 'Kill them! Kill them all!' he bellowed.

Four Dark Elves suddenly sprang from the shadows, their serrated black blades drawn, charging towards Laran, Mother Nature and Solstice.

'You two get out of here!' yelled King Autumn as he turned to face his first attacker, sword drawn.

CHAPTER ELEVEN

King Winter couldn't believe Hyperion had just set Dark Elves on his wife. He would have tried to intervene if he wasn't trapped under Hyperion's control. He realised something else was going on here. Why would Hyperion have so many of those nasty Dark Elves just to take three children hostage? No, there was something else going on. Now that Hyperion had attacked his wife, Taranis was going to make it his business to find out what that was. As for Laran, why else would he be helping Mother Nature when he swore to stay away after Holly? Why had Hyperion taken Laran's son? Lost in his thoughts and growing angrier by the second, Taranis turned his back on the fighting and trudged back to his study.

Lilly and Solstice had escaped, running across the snow-covered lawn back towards their camp. Meanwhile, King Autumn was in the thick of the attack. He thrust his sword into the belly of a Dark Elf, who fell to the floor, dead. Now there were only two Elves remaining. Laran blocked and parried blow after blow with the practised efficiency of a master swordsman. But try as he might, he couldn't find a gap in their defences that would enable him to strike back. He dodged and weaved, retreating out of the hall and outside, past the watching ranks of the Winter Elves and ice creatures, who thankfully didn't seem eager to join in.

Right before Laran was about to defeat his foes, the final Elf quickly slipped his blade in and out of Laran's side, below the protection of his armour. A stabbing pain shot up his side. As he staggered back, he kicked the Elf, and it went stumbling backwards. With all the strength he could muster, he whipped his sword down and across its stomach, causing it to fall to the ground, dead.

Queen Winter and Lilly were waiting in the command tent with Gail when Laran staggered in, clutching the wound at his side. His face was ashen and covered in sweat.

Lilly immediately ran over to him. 'Oh god, Laran. You need a doctor. Gail and I will lead the attack.'

'Just a flesh wound,' he replied, brushing her off. 'Gail, I need you to take the main force of Elven warriors and back up the Sprite's advance. They are going to draw out the hiding ice —' Laran groaned in pain.

'Dad, you're hurt, you need help,' Gail replied.

Laran could feel his vision fading; everything was slowing down.

'You're no use to us like this, Laran. Go to the medical tent. I'll lead the attack,' Lilly ordered, taking charge of the situation.

Laran grunted begrudgingly in agreement. 'Gail and my other lieutenants know what to do. They will take care of the castle defenders. You just focus on getting the children out of there safely.'

'Alright Gail, commence the attack. If Solstice and I are going out there, we need armour,' Lilly commanded with a newfound air of authority.

'Yes, Mother Nature,' Gail replied as he left the tent.

Moments later, the horn sounded, and the battle began.

CHAPTER TWELVE

Andarta sat in her library, poring over one book of her grand collection. She loved books. In fact, her collection, although private, was one of the largest and most important in the world. After all, it was easy to own first editions if you were around when they were originally written. She would never part with any of them and had read them all at least once.

Her favourite genre, however, was romance. She spent countless hours reading and rereading moments of passion, lust, and unrequited love. But she often wondered if love was merely a Human fabrication. She still couldn't fathom its complexities and yearned to feel the comfort of someone who truly understood her.

Moreover, for Andarta not to comprehend something was remarkable. Of the entire Elder Council, her intellect was the keenest. Even Alectrona, with her vast business acumen, was no match. Andarta could work out extremely complex mathematical calculations in her head to a degree of accuracy that would put even the most cutting-edge scientific calculators to shame. She could correctly name any given date of an event, tell you where she was that day, what the weather was like and what she had eaten. Over the years, she had anonymously submitted multiple groundbreaking papers in mathematics, physics, and philosophy. Yet to her immense frustration and sorrow, she had never understood or experienced what true love was like.

She was, of course, hampered by the fact she was immortal and beautiful. She was tall and athletic with fiery, crimson hair. For a long time, she thought she loved Laran. It was only logical. After all, they had been made in pairs, and all the other Kings and Queens of the Elder Council seemed to perfectly complement each other.

It seemed to her that they came in pairs, so they didn't have to be alone. But Laran never reciprocated the love she tried to give him, and she knew that true love wasn't supposed to be one way. She longed for a lover's comfort, but most Humans feared her beauty. She had tried to love mortals in the past, but their lives were so fleeting and the pain of their loss so keen, that she vowed long ago to spare herself the torment. Since then, she concluded that the only people that could ever truly understand or love her were her fellow immortals, namely Laran. It only added to her heartache that over the millennia, they had drifted apart. Aside from their mutual love for Gail, she could no longer find any common ground with him.

Nowadays, she rarely interacted with Humans at all. Of all the Fairy Queens, she was the biggest recluse, spending most of her time in remote Canada. If she wasn't in her library reading her beloved books, she would be in the gym, spending time with Gail or getting lost in the pine forests, enjoying the myriad charms and beauties of nature.

She believed the other council members had abandoned nature as they became more and more tangled up in the affairs of mortals. Indeed, it seemed only Queen Winter still shared her love of the natural world. Although she would never admit it, Andarta was deeply envious of her skills in botany, not to mention the loving relationship she had with Taranis.

Andarta finished reading her book and slumped back in her chair, smiling with satisfaction at its ending: the main character had found her Prince Charming. They were destined to spend the rest of their days in happiness. Good grief, she was lonely.

She looked out the window and listened to the rustling of the trees in the darkness. With a yawn she checked her watch – it was gone midnight; she had been reading uninterrupted for the past five hours. *It was time for bed,* she told herself.

She wandered down the hallway, glancing into Laran's study as she quietly passed by. It was dark and empty. He must be away somewhere. Although he hadn't thought it important enough to tell her. She frowned to herself and climbed the large wooden flight of stairs. She still remembered when the house had first been built. She had designed it – it was a masterpiece of open-plan living with its large rooms and glass walls that looked out onto the gardens surrounding the house.

She wandered into Gail's bedroom and flicked on the light, smiling at the aeroplane wallpaper. She remembered his delight when she had first put it up. Even now, after he was all grown up, he refused to change the wallpaper. He liked its comfort and familiarity. She guessed he was with his dad. Laran had missed him while he was at university. It had amazed her at how Laran had taken to parenthood so keenly. He had never shown any interest in children before, except for that one dark episode in his past.

She walked into her own bedroom and prepared herself for bed. Tomorrow she would get out into the world once more, have some adventures of her own, she told herself as she climbed into bed.

★★★★

Andarta woke the next morning to a still empty house. She was most definitely bored. *So much for getting back into the world*, she thought to herself. She was considering going to get another book to read when the doorbell rang. It was Althea.

'Oh hello. What do you want?' she asked, frowning at the Elf as she opened the door wider so Althea could enter. She showed Althea into the kitchen and offered her something to drink.

Although she didn't show it, she was quite excited to have found this new distraction.

'No thank you, Queen Andarta,' replied Althea.

'Okay,' Andarta replied, before leading her into the lounge and settling on the sofa. Althea sat on a separate sofa and smiled politely.

'I'm afraid you've come at the wrong time, as the boys aren't here right now. But I can pass on a message if you like,' Andarta apologised.

'No, it was you I wanted to speak to.'

'Oh, okay. Go on.' Andarta was surprised. No one ever wanted to talk to her.

Althea paused, not sure how to approach the situation as Althea found Andarta's aloofness hard to handle and she was more than a little intimidated by her.

'Well, Mother Nature is having a bit of trouble with King Winter and King Summer right now. She asked me if I might ask you and Queen Summer to help.'

'Oh, is that so?' Andarta replied, her tone uninterested as she narrowed her eyes at Althea. Althea was beginning to feel uncomfortable, as she was trying to figure out how she was going to convince Andarta to help them. To her relief, however, the phone in the office rang.

Althea waited patiently while Andarta answered the phone. It wasn't long before she returned, her calm composure replaced by a startling resentment.

'Hyperion is indeed back. He's stabbed Laran. I've got to collect him from the hospital. He's in an awful state and the doctors think it will take at least six months before he'll recover. Men are a damn liability, the lot of them,' Andarta scowled as she sat back down on the sofa, her head in her hands. 'I can call Alectrona though and tell her you're coming? She's so busy nowadays, it's almost impossible to pin the damn woman down.'

Althea just smiled and nodded her head politely, careful not to say anything else that might annoy Andarta further.

Althea stayed in the lounge with her hands in her lap as Andarta went to her office to call Alectrona. After a while, Althea felt quite bored and started glancing around the room. The lounge was large and spacious, with a clear view of the garden and woods beyond it. There was a large, fluffy rug on the floor and an antique grand piano in the corner. The room was dotted with pictures of Laran, Gail, and Andarta. Althea smiled. Some pictures were of Gail when he was a child. She was about to explore the house further when Andarta reappeared.

'I've phoned ahead. They'll be expecting you,' she informed Althea as she strode over. 'Now you really have to leave, as I've got to go to England and collect Laran.'

'Thank you for your time,' Althea replied courteously as Andarta escorted her out of the door.

'Goodbye!' she called merrily over her shoulder, quite relieved to be out of her presence as she crossed the garden towards the woods. She chose the best tree and placed her palm against it until the shimmering door appeared. She thought of Alectrona's house, and was immediately transported to a small house, flanked by brightly coloured flower beds. Alectrona stood on her doorstep, smiling warmly at the Elf.

'Althea darling, how are you? Please come in,' she said as she led Althea into her home. 'Now then. Tell me what's going on. I had

Laran here just the other day asking for help, but I thought he was just overreacting. You know how he can sulk. But now Andarta is telling me that blithering idiot husband of mine has injured him. God, I feel guilty. He's going to be laid up in bed for the next six months. How will poor Andarta cope? Anyway, you come into the sitting room and get yourself comfy sweetie, whilst I fix you a nice, warm drink.'

A little while later, she returned with a cup of tea for herself and, much to Althea's delight, a hot chocolate for Althea. Althea took it with a smile.

'There you go, dear. I know it's your favourite. Now, tell me everything from the beginning.'

And so Althea told her every single detail, shocking Alectrona completely.

'That's dreadful! Laran didn't mention any of this when he was here. Silly boy. I'll accompany you to Scotland or there's no telling what my half-wit of a husband will do next.'

CHAPTER THIRTEEN

Taranis was fuming. What was King Summer thinking? Setting those wicked things on his wife was the last straw. He watched in horror from the safety of his study as Solstice and Lilly ran across the lawn to the cover of the trees whilst Laran fought back desperately, ending up with a serious injury.

King Winter was afraid of Laran, and if he was going to extricate himself from this mess, which he had been stupid enough to get tangled up in, he would have to act fast. He stood up and paced the room. He put his hands in his pocket and felt the cold metal form of a key. Oh yes, with all the drama he had forgotten about the children! Perhaps he would check on them.

As King Winter walked down the corridor, his spirits lifted slightly. Maybe the children could be his way out of all this. Had he just thought that? To try and use the children as his own bargaining chip? Sometimes his cowardliness disgusted even himself.

He placed his ear to the door – he couldn't hear anything from inside. Only a horn blowing far off in the distance. As he slowly opened the door, William, who was still holding the fire poker, confronted him. King Winter grabbed it before William could use it. He wasn't quick enough, however, to avoid William's other fist, which hit him square in the face.

'What do you want?' demanded Willow, glaring at King Winter, who had staggered backwards and fallen to the floor, his nose pouring with blood.

'I came to see if you were alright,' King Winter moaned as he climbed to his feet and raised his hands to show he meant no harm in case William tried to attack him again. 'Please don't hit me again. That really hurt,' he said, looking at William.

'What do you care how we are? You kidnapped us,' William replied angrily. The boy was as tall as Taranis and a lot broader. Taranis had the impression that William would be more than happy to hit him again. In that moment, he was rather relieved the other boy had escaped, as he wasn't sure he could handle two angry teenage boys.

'Yes, I know. I'm sorry. I didn't think it would get this far,' King Winter apologised. King Summer was right. The boy reminded him of someone, but he just couldn't remember who.

'Are you hungry? You must be — you've been in here for so long. I can take you to the kitchen.' King Winter tried to sound friendly and gave them his best smile.

'Why are you being nice?' asked Willow suspiciously, narrowing her eyes at him.

'It might be a trick,' William signed to Willow so King Winter wouldn't understand.

'I don't think so,' she signed back.

'Okay,' Willow addressed Taranis. 'But we want to know where our Mum is. She said she was coming right back.'

'There was a complication. She had to leave for a little while, but she'll be back soon, don't worry,' he blurted as he escorted them to the kitchen, where he watched them silently make sandwiches.

Once they had finished, he walked them back to their room. 'I want you to stay away from the window no matter what you see or hear, alright?' King Winter said as he backed out the door.

'Why? What's going on? You can't keep us locked in here forever!' Willow shouted back, but Taranis just ignored her.

He shut the door and locked it, putting the key safely back in his pocket. Now all he had to do was find Mother Nature before King Autumn destroyed his castle entirely.

Lilly watched from the top of the hill as the battle began. Gail had taken charge of King Autumn's forces and was launching the attack on the castle with Queen Winter.

First, he sent the Tree Sprites. With their gangly legs and sharp, wooden fingers, the Sprites attacked the ice giants. But their fingers were no use against the ice giants, who were almost smashing them to pieces. Luckily, the Sprites were able to dart and weave their way out of reach before the giants could do them more harm.

In the meantime, King Autumn's Warrior Elves charged into battle, bypassing the ice giants, heading straight for the Winter Elves. It was chaos. The vicious, fur-covered snowmen slashed and stabbed at the Autumn Elves with their claws and swords. But the Elves proved themselves skilful warriors and maintained the upper hand.

But they weren't the only weapons in King Autumn's arsenal. Soon, Forest Golems joined the pack. With trunk-like arms and broad chests, these yellow-eyed creatures were formidable fighters. Coming to the aid of the Sprites, the ice giants were defeated.

Queen Winter walked up the hill towards Lilly, decked in Winter Elf's armour.

'We must enter the castle now,' Solstice commanded, surveying the battle below. 'If we wait until the battle is over, Hyperion might hurt the children. How will we get through? Can you blast them with sunlight?'

'Not at this distance. It isn't accurate enough, and it drains me. I can't appear weak.'

'We will clear the way for you, Mother Nature. Let's go now!' Gail called over to them.

'Wait!' Solstice said quickly. 'There is a side door that is rarely locked. That could be our best way in.'

'Yes! That's the one I used to escape the castle.' Gail nodded in agreement.

'Okay, you lead the way. Gail, you and your men bring up the rear,' instructed Lilly as she followed Solstice down the hill and around the back of the castle, where there was little resistance. What an oversight.

Solstice tried the door, finding it was indeed unlocked. *Sometimes*, she thought to herself, *I loved that dim-witted husband of mine*. They all hurried inside to the empty corridor of the castle.

'Where to now?' asked Lilly, looking nervously down the corridor.

'My husband's office,' replied Queen Winter. 'If he's hiding somewhere, that's where he'll be.' She led the way, striding purposefully down the corridor.

King Summer stood by one window, his hands clasped tightly behind his back as he watched the battle below. Of course, King Winter's troops were losing. Damn it, why was that man so useless? The five remaining Dark Elves were with him, skulking silently in the background. *We can't stay here*, he thought. He could take the children to his apartment in Dubai. No, that would never work. It was part of a large apartment complex and there were too many Human staff for the children to be held unnoticed. His only other choice was to turn them over to the King of the Dark Elves. But first, he had to get out of here. He was going to use the children to make sure that he did.

'You there!' he commanded, turning to one of the Dark Elves. 'Fetch the children. We're leaving immediately!'

'Yes, King Summer,' the creature replied, before vanishing into the shadows. A moment later, it returned empty-handed.

King Summer raised his eyebrow in frustration. 'Well, where are they?' he demanded irritably.

'My apologies, my Lord, but the children are locked in. I cannot get to them.'

'Well, where's the key?' Hyperion asked, before groaning with impatience. 'Find King Winter.'

'Yes, my Lord.'

Hyperion went back to watching the battle unfold, before deciding he was bored with the life-or-death struggle, which was taking place just metres from where he stood. Turning on his heel, he walked back towards the great hall.

Queen Winter barged into her husband's office. On seeing Queen Winter, Taranis abruptly tried to stand up, but Gail already had a sword at his throat.

'My dear, how good to see you and Mother Nature,' King Winter croaked in his most congenial voice under Gail's sword. 'No King Autumn, I am surprised. And I'm not sure I have met all these gentlemen, but Gail, it's good to see you unharmed.'

'Shut up Taranis and give me the key to the children's room now,' demanded Lilly. 'What happened to your nose?' she asked, suddenly noticing Taranis's swollen and bleeding nose.

'That boy of yours is quite the little ruffian. He punched me. You really should teach him better manners,' King Winter complained, trying to get up. 'Do you mind?' he said to Gail, who was still holding his sword to Taranis's throat. Gail looked at Lilly, who nodded her head, and he lowered the sword.

'Thank you,' said Taranis, finally getting up. 'Shall we?' he said, gesturing towards the door.

'Gail, take his arm and hold that sword by his side. If he tries anything – anything at all – run it through him,' said Lilly in her coldest voice. She ignored the glare that Queen Winter gave her as they marched King Winter down the corridor to the children's room.

It was on the way to the children's room that a Dark Elf appeared. On seeing them with King Winter, he turned to run and immediately shouted for help. Moments later, four more appeared out of the shadows with their weapons drawn. They approached slowly, ready for battle.

Gail and his four men immediately formed a protective barrier between the Dark Elves and Mother Nature, abandoning King Winter.

'You go no further; those children are in the custody of King Summer. Hand over the key, or we shall force it from you,' rasped one of the Dark Elves.

King Winter backed away slowly. 'I think I'll return to my study for a bit,' he mumbled.

But after seeing Queen Winter's venomous glare, he changed his mind.

'Queen Winter, is there another way to the children?' Lilly shouted to Solstice as Gail and his honour guard attacked the Dark Elves.

'Yes, but it leads through the main hall. Let's go!' Solstice called back. They raced down the corridor towards the main hall, dragging King Winter with them.

But Gail and his guards were struggling. The Dark Elves could move through the shadows unseen and began rapidly vanishing and reappearing to dodge Gail and his men's attacks. Already, two of Gail's guard had fallen to the Dark Elves. A third one cried out as a Dark Elf appeared behind him and stabbed him in the back. With a snarl, Gail swung his blade towards the Dark Elf's throat, but he only sliced through thick, purple smoke.

CHAPTER FOURTEEN

Queen Winter, Lilly and King Winter entered the main hall to find King Summer caressing a long, curved blade. He raised his sword, pointing the tip at King Winter.

'Give me the key,' Hyperion commanded as he strode towards King Winter.

'Give up, Hyperion, it's over,' he said rather unconvincingly. 'Laran's troops are winning the battle. His second in command is beating your Dark Elf lackeys, and we have the key to the children's room. Face it. You've lost,' he finished as Hyperion stopped less than a foot away, lowering his sword.

But at that moment, the Dark Elf leader appeared. 'My lord, King Autumn's warriors are defeated, and we have captured their leader.'

'Excellent!' King Summer beamed and, without warning, stabbed King Winter in the stomach. Taranis looked at King Summer in shock as he sunk to the floor, clutching his abdomen.

'No!' Queen Winter shrieked, starting towards her husband, only to be stopped at sword point by King Summer.

'Such is the fate of all traitors,' King Summer sneered, raising his voice over the sound of the blizzard outside. King Summer retrieved a key from Taranis's pocket and threw it at the Dark Elf. 'Fetch the children. It's time to do some bargaining,' he said with a smile. Lilly stared at him in horror.

William stood back from the bedroom door as three Dark Elves barged in. He held the fire poker and signalled to Willow to get behind him.

'You will come with us, Human,' the lead Elf declared.

'We are not to leave this room,' William replied defiantly.

'Do you want us to force you?' the Elf sneered, moving toward William.

The Dark Elves pulled William, Willow, and their Guardian Elves out of the room and into the hall. Shortly after, Gail was dragged in, his face bruised and beaten.

'Now, Mother Nature, maybe you'd like to cooperate? If not, these Dark Elves will kill these youths one by one, starting with Laran's Elf.' Hyperion was relieved – finally things were going according to plan.

'I will not bow to your insanity, Hyperion,' replied Lilly angrily.

'Of course you won't. But who will help you now? Did Laran get bored? Thought he could just send his Elf to do his work for him?' Hyperion smiled. He knew exactly what had happened to Laran. With him out of the way, Lilly had to realise they outmatched her.

He gave a curt nod to the Dark Elves, and two of them roughly took hold of Gail and pulled him forward. William tried to kick one of them in the shin, only to be rewarded by a hard slap across the face.

'Got spirit, hasn't he? Does he get that from you or his father?'

'Leave them alone, Hyperion. This is between you and me.' Lilly glared at him.

One of the Dark Elves stepped on the back of Gail's calf, forcing him to kneel. The Elf then grabbed a handful of his hair, forcing his head back and exposing his throat. It then pressed its sword against Gail's throat and dragged it across. It was a shallow wound, but Gail started bleeding profusely. He didn't flinch or make a sound, staring defiantly at King Summer.

'Stop Hyperion!' Lilly cried.

'No.' Hyperion nodded to the Dark Elf that was holding William. The Dark Elf dragged him forward and forced him to his knees. The one holding Gail pressed the sword deeper into the cut as more blood oozed from the wound. A look of pain briefly flashed across his face, and the Dark Elf grinned menacingly, desperate to finish the job. William cried out in shock and pain. Lilly looked at William with concern. Why was he behaving so strangely? What had made him cry out like that? The Elf holding him hadn't harmed him yet. Then she suddenly realised what had been nagging at the back of her mind for weeks now. Her whole body went stiff with terror. If she was correct – and she suspected she was – they would be in even more trouble than she had originally thought.

'Wait, just wait!' Lilly shouted. 'I can compromise.'

'Mum, no!' Willow sobbed.

'Release them, Hyperion. I will reconsider.'

Hyperion snapped his fingers, and the Dark Elves dropped the two boys to the ground. 'Where shall I begin? First, call off your troops outside,' he commanded as he settled into Taranis's throne. 'I want you to give me all of your power and authority so I can sort out this Human issue myself. Then you and your adorable children can go back to your boring, insignificant life. Actually, forget that. I'll make you a list.' Hyperion rambled as he pondered over his demands. But that was all right with Lilly. Her very last option was to play for time and hope the help she was waiting for arrived soon...

At that moment, the front doors were blasted open so suddenly that King Summer carried on speaking for half a second before he registered the noise.

Beams of sunlight, which shone through the windows, and motes of dust swirling through the air replaced the howling winds outside. And to everyone's surprise, little Althea trotted in, looking rather pleased with herself, followed by Aaron and his men. The Dark Elves started rounding in on them before they saw someone else behind them, silhouetted by the bright sunshine. The mysterious figure raised an arm and blasted each of them into dust with a ray of pure sunlight as everyone watched on in shock.

'Ugh, not you. What do you want? This is none of your concern. Don't you have better things to do?' Hyperion said, exasperated yet bewildered by this shocking turn of events.

'Oh, shut up, Hyperion,' replied a woman's voice. An elegant, tall, blonde woman stepped out of the sunlight into clearer view.

'Oh, Ali! I'm so glad to see you!' Lilly cried in delight.

'Well, when I heard what this cretin was up to, I dropped everything. I'm sorry I took so long,' Alectrona, Queen of the Summer Elves, replied, shooting King Summer a very stern look. She strode towards the throne where King Summer sat. 'Give me that,' she demanded, snatching the sword from him and chucking it to the floor. 'Do you have any idea how busy I've been while you,' she said, poking him in the chest, 'have been acting like a complete fool? Laran will be laid up for the next six months because of you. And Good Heavens!

What on earth have you done to Gail?' Alectrona turned to face the poor boy whose neck was now tinted red with blood. 'You've been in self-declared exile for fifty years and this is how you announce your return? What is wrong with you, Hyperion?' Alectrona sighed and turned to face everyone else in the hall. 'I will take him to FERA. Lord Hurleston has a lot of questions for him. I'll make sure he won't be bothering any of you again.'

King Summer looked completely miserable as Alectrona raised a hand and two of Aaron's men came forward to stand on either side of the throne.

'No...' King Summer grumbled feebly.

'Pardon?'

'I said no!' King Summer argued back, finding his voice once again. 'How dare you talk to me like that. Have you forgotten who I am? I am the King of the Summer Elves, foremost and most powerful of the Elder Council. I was the first to unite you all against the tyranny that came before, and it was I that led you all to victory and got us where we are now. You think you can just come in here and give me a stern slapping on the wrist, like I'm one of her brats?' King Summer spat, glaring at Lilly.

'Yes, I can,' she replied, and she lowered her voice when she spoke again, 'and if you don't come quietly, I will force your cooperation.'

'With a flick of my wrist, I can reduce this entire castle to ash!' Hyperion was bellowing maniacally now. He was like a baby throwing all its toys out of the pram.

'Go on then, I'd love to see it. Frankly, I'm wondering why, if you're so great, you seem to need more power than you already have.'

'I mean it. I will.' Hyperion's face was growing red with anger.

'We know. We're waiting to see it.'

'You all brought this on yourselves!' Hyperion yelled before he stood from his throne and began gritting his teeth, his face going to an even darker shade of crimson.

For a moment, William thought he felt a slight tingling feeling on his arm.

The hall was plunged into silence as nothing happened. Hyperion shouted in frustration, and Alectrona gave him a look of pity.

'You see, what you've forgotten, honey, is that you derive your power from doing your duties as King. The same duties you've neglected and left me to do for the last fifty years, meaning I have all your power now. I could probably easily fry everyone in this room. But you would probably struggle to melt an ice cube.'

'No, this can't be! This is wrong, all wrong!' Hyperion stammered. He tried to run out of the hall, but Aaron's men grabbed him. Alectrona stood there, smiling to herself as she watched him struggle against them.

'Aren't you going to go after him?' Gail asked as a medic from the Autumn Army examined his neck and throat.

'I can't be bothered, Gail.' Queen Summer laughed. 'Oh yes, that reminds me. Gail dear, will you be running things while King Autumn is indisposed?'

'Yes, I expect so.'

'Wonderful. I'll drop by and have a coffee with your Mum soon. See you then, sweetie. Lilly, we must do lunch darling! And Solstice, sorry about the mess.' She gave a small, friendly wave to William and Willow before she left, almost as soon as she had arrived.

William watched the medics take King Winter away to the waiting air ambulance with Queen Winter. The bright sunlight had nearly melted all the snow and snow creatures. Things were slowly returning to normal.

Willow stood in the main hall with Lilly. 'Wow! She was efficient. Shame she wasn't here earlier,' Willow laughed, giving her Mum a hug.

'Right, shall we go home? I could do with a cup of tea,' Lilly replied.

'Mother Nature, would you be so kind as to excuse me? I must return to camp,' Gail asked. His neck was now covered in a bandage.

'Of course, and Gail, thank you so much for all your help. I'm sorry for your losses, and I hope Laran will make a full recovery. Oh, let's meet next week?' Lilly said with a warm smile.

'Thank you, ma'am,' he said as he hurried out through the destroyed oak doors. He stopped on the step that William was sitting on.

'Are you okay, William?'

William quickly stood up, not realising any-one was there. 'Yeah, sorry. I'm alright.'

Gail rummaged in his pocket and passed William his phone for him to put in his number.

'We're linked, William. I'll be in touch.' Gail politely held out his hand and William took it. 'Friends?' Gail asked tentatively.

'Absolutely,' William grinned back

Just then, Willow interrupted them. 'Gail!' she called, running over. 'Thank you for rescuing us!' She smiled shyly and gave him a hug. As she stepped back, she caught sight of William smirking at her. *Out of your league,* he mouthed at her. Gail gave a small wave at the pair of them before hurrying on his way.

'He looked so fit in that armour,' Willow said longingly, making Lilly roll her eyes.

'How are we getting home?' asked William.

'By tree,' answered Lilly.

'Ugh, do we have to? I hate travelling by tree. Why can't we use the train like normal people?' complained William.

'What, dressed like this?' replied Lilly. 'You are joking.'

'Excuse me, Ma'am, King Winter has a helicopter on the roof. I could find a pilot to take you home,' one soldier informed them politely.

'Oh. That would be very kind, thank you, but I don't wish to cause any trouble.'

'No trouble. I don't think it'd be safe to use the trees until we have rounded all the Dark Elves up,' he explained before hurrying to find a pilot.

It just so happened that Gail was the only one who could take them home. Upon landing, Lilly asked Gail to come inside for tea.

'No, I shouldn't come in. I must get back.' Gail smiled regretfully. He would have liked to have spoken to Willow some more.

'Okay. I'll see you next week at work then. Thanks again, Gail.'

They stepped out of the helicopter and watched Gail ascend back into the sky and across the fields away from them.

'I didn't realise the Elder Council had children,' Willow said, watching the helicopter become a small dot and eventually vanish behind the clouds.

Yeah Mum, William thought to himself sarcastically, *and I'm the one linked to one of them. I wonder what else you're hiding from me.* William trudged ahead inside, not bothering to wait for the others.

'Yes, some of them do. I believe King Spring has a couple,' Lilly said, glancing at her daughter with amusement. 'Gail's a very polite young man.'

'I bet he has a girlfriend, though,' Willow answered sadly.

CHAPTER FIFTEEN

Gail stepped out of the lift and walked up the corridor to Hàlfr's office.

'Gail, how are you?' Hàlfr asked politely as Gail knocked on the door and pushed it open.

'Fine, thanks,' Gail replied, trying desperately to sound a little less miserable than he truly was. Why couldn't he decide? All he had to do was ask… but what if she said no? What if he had read the situation all wrong? She was just a girl; how hard could this be?

'Are you sure? You don't sound it,' Hàlfr replied.

Gail looked at him, unsure whether Hàlfr would be interested, but decided to tell him anyway – he had to talk to someone other than his Mum. 'So, I met this girl…' Gail managed, feeling embarrassed already. Hàlfr raised an eyebrow.

'The thing is, I want to see her again, but I don't know if I should.' Gail was wishing he had said nothing now. 'I don't know if it was the circumstances of our meeting and if I'm reading more into it than there actually is.'

Hàlfr looked at Gail, seeing the boy, not the intelligence officer. Hàlfr knew exactly which girl had attracted Gail's attention. 'I'm guessing this girl is Child of Nature, who you met recently?'

Gail nodded sheepishly.

'That's my boy! Aim high,' Hàlfr joked until he noticed Gail looked even more miserable. Hàlfr composed himself and thought of a more serious response.

'Just get her number and call her. Ask her if she wants to go for a coffee. If she says yes, you're in. If not, oh well, you gave it a shot, and move on to the next. Life's too short to be messing around and acting all shy all the time. Nothing ventured, nothing gained, after all.'

Gail wasn't convinced. *Easy for him to say*, he said to himself. He talks to everyone. He picked up some reports and tried to read them, shuffling them in his hands before putting them back on the desk, defeated. There hadn't ever been a first girl, never mind a next one. He was miserable again.

'There isn't likely to be a next one though, is there?' Gail blurted out suddenly.

'What do you mean?' Hàlfr asked, realising Gail had been bottling all this up for a while now.

'Well, no one would dare date King Autumn's son, would they? I can't relate to anyone because I've been brought up in the Human world, but I can't socialise with Humans because I'm an Elf and my parents are immortal royalty,' Gail replied gloomily. 'I was fifteen when I got into Harvard, a child genius basically. No girl was going to even look at me.' Gail felt a blush staining his skin. 'Sorry I don't know why I said all that, just forget I said anything.' He tried to smile.

Hàlfr was stunned as he looked at the crumpled boy before him. 'Well, there you go. Child of Nature won't care about any of that, so you're in with quite a good chance. Just text her Gail,' Hàlfr smiled. Gail nodded and turned his attention back to the intelligence reports.

'But what if she has a boyfriend already?' Gail blurted out again.

'Okay Gail, what is this all about? What's really bothering you?' Hàlfr asked gently, putting down the reports he was holding.

'I don't know really,' Gail lapsed into silence, hanging his head.

Hàlfr waited patiently.

'It's just they were so nice to me at the castle, and they didn't have to be. I'm tired Hàlfr. Tired of hiding, of being King Autumn's son, of being Lord Aristata. I just want to be me and have friends and be normal. I'm tired of all this being on my own.'

Hàlfr studied Gail slumped in his chair. He looked like a normal teenager, not the soldier nor the intelligence officer Laran was training him to be.

'Gail, just message her. If she doesn't want to date you, you'll get over it. Just be friends with them. They don't care whose son you are.'

'Thanks, Hàlfr.' Gail stood up decisively and picked up the reports. 'And you know all this spy business?'

'What about it?' Hàlfr looked at Gail, wondering where he was going with this.

'I think it might be Carol, Lord Hurleston's secretary.'

'Really? What makes you say that?' Hàlfr asked, intrigued. He had some theories about Carol himself.

'I don't have any hard evidence. But there are little things I've noticed. And she's perfectly placed. She has been here so long she's almost above suspicion.'

'Okay, I'll monitor her,' Hàlfr thanked Gail.

Lilly was sitting in her office, finishing the mountain of paperwork that the siege at the castle had generated. She would remember this next time Laran tried to persuade her to go into battle. As she signed the last form and closed her file, there was a polite knock on the door. Lilly opened the door to find Gail outside.

'Gail, come in. Take a seat.' She couldn't help but notice the bandage still around his neck. 'Can I get you anything?' she asked.

'No thank you, Mother Nature. What did you want to speak to me about?'

Lilly sat back behind her desk and studied the young man in front of her. 'You must call me Lilly. I believe we're going to be working together closely over the coming months, but that isn't why I invited you here today.' Lilly took a deep breath and carried on. 'Gail, I noticed something at the castle that I think could have a detrimental effect on you and my son, if it is widely known. I need to know who else knows.' She hoped he understood what she was referring to.

'I assume you're referring to my link with William?' Lilly nodded and Gail continued, 'No one knows, only King and Queen Autumn. Dad has always gone out of his way to keep it like that. He was always worried they could use it against you or me or even him. Not even the Elder Council knows. Mum and Dad especially kept it a secret from them, although I'm not sure about Aunty Alectrona. I mean, Queen Summer.'

'I see.' It was strange hearing him talk about his family; Lilly had never thought of them in those terms. 'Right, yes, your father is right. We should keep this to ourselves. But while you are running his office, you will report directly to me, okay? Just to keep you safe and to make sure nothing untoward is going on. I'm not checking up on you. It's just, well, I don't want you getting hurt because William is careless,' Lilly said reassuringly.

'Will that be all?' Gail asked, slightly relieved. It had always bothered him that Mother Nature had been kept in the dark regarding the link. But why hadn't he told her that Willow and William know? Something in him held that information back, almost like a pact between them. *You're being daft*, he told himself.

'Yes, thank you Gail. Are you coming down to the infirmary to see Andarta before she takes Laran home?'

'No, I have some errands to run for Lord Hurleston and then I have some leave. So, I'm going home to help Mum – sorry, I mean Andarta – after that.'

'Gail, do you know why you are linked to William?' Lilly suddenly asked.

Gail nervously swallowed and replied, 'No, I don't. I wasn't aware of it until recently. My parents told me one day after I passed out.'

'Oh, goodness. I am sorry if William caused you any embarrassment,' Lilly apologised.

Gail chuckled in response. 'It's alright. He got quite drunk…'

'Oh, Tom's party last summer. Yes, he was very ill,' Lilly replied, stifling a laugh. 'I do apologise for my son.'

'But Mum and Dad have always known. Mum is worried about it because she doesn't trust the Elder Council. I asked them, and they were a bit vague. They said they didn't want to worry me unduly or something like that. Although my paternal aunt was your mother's Elf. I kind of assumed it was some sort of family tradition.' Gail shrugged apologetically. He was going to press them further when he got home.

'Thanks Gail,' Lilly nodded to him as she stood up to let him out. She tried to mask the shock of his revelation as it pushed forward all those childhood memories in her mind.

'Um Lilly… Could I ask a favour?' Gail hovered at the door, biting his lip nervously.

'Yes, of course.' Lilly was honestly glad of the distraction from her swirling emotions.

'Could I have Willow's phone number?' he said in a rush. 'Of course, you don't have to, I mean… if that's okay?' His face had gone a deep shade of crimson.

'Oh, of course,' Lilly replied, taking her phone out of her pocket and schooling her features so as not to embarrass the boy any further.

She watched him go and couldn't help thinking about what Gail had said about her mother's Elf being an aunt of his.

CHAPTER SIXTEEN

King Summer sat at a plain metal table. He was in an interview room, the sort you would see on a detective program. It was small with bare walls, except for a two-way mirror, which covered one of them. On top of the table sat a tape recorder.

He hadn't been waiting long before the door opened, and Lord Hurleston walked in. He sat down at the table in front of King Summer, clasped his hands in front of him, and smiled.

'King Summer, how did you end up in a place like this?' Hurleston said. He had never met King Summer before and was struggling to size him up.

'I could destroy you for your insolence. You can't cage me here like some sort of dirty animal!'

'But you can't destroy me, can you? You've lost all your power. You're out of shape,' Hurleston replied simply.

'What do you want from me? Are you looking to torment me?'

'No, ironically. I'm here to figure out why *you're* here. So, what drove you into my custody, Hyperion?' Hurleston replied, completely unfazed by Hyperion's attempts to intimidate him.

'Necessity,' King Summer responded coldly.

'Excuse me?'

'Necessity brought me here, Human. It was necessary that I acted the way I did, and I do not regret it.'

'You mean to say that it was necessary to kidnap children?' Hurleston asked, bewildered by this response.

'You're not seeing the bigger picture. I had to use Mother Nature to launch the first strike, to begin the attack.'

'Attack? Against whom? Humanity? Why do you get to decide if we live or die?'

'I didn't, you decided for yourselves. I gave you all the warnings. You ignore the signs I have shown you. As a species, you choose to do nothing. Granted, it's all happening rather more quickly than I would have imagined, but that's because you have no natural predators, nothing to stop the population. I could provide you with an enemy to fight and you would both fight bitterly, losing thousands, even millions, between you. But the Elder Council has done that before and to be frank, it's boring now. Either I can force you to change or I can not. I can wait until you've abused this Earth completely to watch you turn on each other. I know which one will be slower, which one will be the cruellest. I've watched your species grow for millions of years, but I can't watch that.'

'But there must be another way, a better solution,' Hurleston insisted.

'Is there? I've been looking for it for the last fifty years and I've come up with nothing.'

'Well, I refuse to accept yours; we're getting smarter. Eco-friendly cities are already being developed. We're better at recycling. We're already changing for the better and I think we'd sooner pull together and fix this planet rather than driving ourselves to extinction,' Hurleston argued.

'All seven billion of you? Deciding to do what's right instead of what's easy? Please! Do I look stupid? I've seen great things during my lifetime, but I assure you I won't live to see that. You'll fail, again and again and again, like you always have.'

'You have no power, Hyperion. You pose no threat.'

'That's where you're wrong. Do you think all my power just vanished? I used it up. I over-exerted. I needed to recharge, but I couldn't. I had to hold *them* in check to buy you time in case there was something I had overlooked. In the smallest hope that I had missed some-thing, that I was wrong. But I'm not wrong, am I?' King Summer leaned forward, invading Hurleston's personal space.

'What were you holding in check? What's really been going on here?' Hurleston pressed him, holding his stare.

'I used to help him, you know. We used to fight them together. But of course, he only ever fought them out of hatred. Unlike me, he never grew tired, he never wondered why.'

'Who never wondered why? Who were you fighting?'

'The Dark Elves, of course. They have been preparing for open war against the Humans for years. Now they are ready to come out of the shadows and overthrow humanity to become the dominant race. Your species is at war and the Dark Elves have already made their first move!'

END OF BOOK 2